D0949589

BILLY SURE

·KID ENTREPRENEUR·

AND THE ATTACK OF THE MYSTERIOUS LUNCH MEAT

INVENTED BY **LUKE SHARPE**

DRAWINGS BY **GRAHAM ROSS**

Simon Spotlight

New York   London   Toronto   Sydney   New Delhi

SIMON SPOTLIGHT
An imprint of Simon & Schuster Children's Publishing Division
1230 Avenue of the Americas, New York, New York 10020
This Simon Spotlight hardcover edition May 2017
Copyright © 2017 by Simon & Schuster, Inc. Text by Michael Teitelbaum.
Illustrations by Graham Ross. All rights reserved, including the right of reproduction in whole or in part in any form.
SIMON SPOTLIGHT and colophon are registered trademarks of Simon & Schuster, Inc.
For information about special discounts for bulk purchases, please contact Simon & Schuster Special Sales at 1-866-506-1949 or business@simonandschuster.com.
Designed by Jay Colvin
The text of this book was set in Minya Nouvelle.
Manufactured in the United States of America 0417 FFG
10 9 8 7 6 5 4 3 2 1
ISBN 978-1-4814-7910-3 (hc)
ISBN 978-1-4814-7909-7 (pbk)
ISBN 978-1-4814-7911-0 (eBook)
Library of Congress Catalog Card Number 2016940855

Chapter One

Eighth Grade!

YOU KNOW THAT FIRST DAY OF SCHOOL FEELING? THAT one where on the outside you seem calm and relaxed, but on the inside you're feeling a little nervous? Yeah, that feeling—the feeling that everything is about to change—that's how I felt last year.

My name is Billy Sure, and last year I became kind of a celebrity. If you haven't heard my name by now, I'm the **CEO** and inventor in charge of **SURE THINGS, INC.** I run the company along with my best friend Manny Reyes, who is our super smart CFO, businessperson, marketing person, and all-around numbers guy.

My life in the past year has been a pretty crazy ride. I've invented all kinds of things, like the CANDY TOOTHBRUSH, SIBLING SILENCER, CAT-DOG TRANSLATOR, and the ALL BALL. I also got to work on a secret mission for spies, be part of a few reality TV shows, and make friends with lots of cool celebrities!

So you'd think something as simple as the first day of eighth grade wouldn't give me the first day of school jitters, right? WRONG. I may be starting eighth grade off right—with my best friends at my side, my invention company doing well, and texting a girl I kind of like—but deep down I'm just a regular kid who thinks the first day of school is plain SCARY!

"Don't forget," says Mr. Jennings, my new history teacher as he erases the whiteboard, "chapters one through four are due tomorrow."

Yikes! Homework? On the *first day of school?* Sounds like Emily was right—she said eighth grade would be harder than seventh, and I've *already* got tons of homework to do.

Emily is my older sister, by the way. She's a sophomore in high school now. I used to think high schoolers were cool . . . but now I don't even want to *think* about the amount of homework they get.

BRIIIIIIING!

The bell rings. As I hurry down the hall to my next class—science—I get an incoming text from Jada Parikh. Remember when I said I'm texting a girl I kind of like? Okay, okay, that's Jada Parikh. Jada is also part of Sure Things, Inc.'s rival invention company, Definite Devices. I guess that should have made us enemies or something, but we are actually pretty good friends. Jada's amazing at video games and she's the number three *Sandbox XXL* player IN THE ENTIRE WORLD!

I open Jada's text. It's a picture of her beating a *Sandbox XXL* mini game in record time.

Scratch that.

NUMBER TWO PLAYER IN THE ENTIRE WORLD!

Jada doesn't go to my school, Fillmore Middle School. She goes to private school and they don't start their classes until next week. But we live pretty close to each other and know lots of the same people. She and Petula Brown are on the same foosball travel league, for example.

As I slip into science class, I notice that Ms. Soo has already placed a list of the labs we're expected to complete this quarter on the board.

No doubt about it. Eighth grade is no joke!

Ms. Soo outlines the way the year will go. Chemistry readings, lectures, labs. Biology experiments, films, field trips. A physics conference with the eighth grade advanced math class, demonstrating the connection between the two subjects.

My head is starting to SPIN. But at least she hasn't given us any homework on the first day of school.

"And here is your homework assignment for tonight," Ms. Soo says, as if my thought had jinxed it!

Rats. I add that assignment to my growing list labeled HOW IN THE WORLD WILL BILLY SURE GET ALL OF THIS DONE?!

BRIIIIIIING!

The bell rings again. As it does, I see Timothy Bu and Clayton Harris looking up at each other and shaking their heads. At least I'm not the only one surprised by all of this homework!

Next up is lunch. Thankfully, I won't have to worry about lunch—even eighth grade lunch.

Not unless the cafeteria staff assigns me homework, anyway!

In the cafeteria I sit with a bunch of my friends at a long table. We're a pretty interesting group. Manny sits next to me. Around the rest of the table sits Petula Brown, Peter MacHale, Allison Arnolds, Timothy Bu, Samantha Jenkins, and Clayton Harris.

For a long time Manny and I tried to make it a point not to sit together at lunch. We spend so much time together at Sure Things, Inc. that we thought it would be a good idea to hang out with other friends at lunchtime. But now all of our friends like to hang out together. It's pretty GREAT, if I do say so myself!

I open the brown bag Dad packed for me. My dad likes to cook, though his food creations are a little . . . um, *creative*, I should say. In my brown bag I find one of his trademark PEANUT-BUTTER-AND-JELLY-STUFFED PICKLES. They actually taste better than they sound.

Like me, Manny brings his own lunch to

school every day. He takes out a turkey sandwich in the shape of what can only be someone's
foot. There are little pieces of cheese on what
should be the foot's toenails. I guess that makes
sense—Manny's mom, Dr. Reyes, is a podiatrist,
and sometimes she takes her job a *little* too
seriously. Or maybe she gets a KICK out of it?

The rest of our friends buy their lunch in the cafeteria. They sit with trays of food in front of them.

"How was everyone's summer?" I ask, a typical first-day-back-at-school question.

"I made some serious cash mowing lawns," says Peter. "I'm saving up to get a really awesome mountain bike. It will be the *cooooolest!*"

If you ask Peter, everything he has or does is the "*cooooolest!*"

"I had a pretty good time at camp. Then I had to work at my family's fancy restaurant," Allison says. "I spent a lot of my summer saying stuff like, 'Would you like the *elite* set of silverware or the *royal* set of silverware, sir?'"

We all laugh.

Timothy pokes at whatever is on his tray. "I ran every day," he says. "This year I'm going to make the school track team. Did you know that it takes five hundred twenty-five steps to go around the track *one* time? I counted."

Oh yeah. Timothy's hobby is counting steps.

Told you I have some interesting friends.

"I worked with my mom this summer at *Right Next Door*," Samantha says cheerfully.

Right Next Door is our local online newspaper. Samantha's mom, Kathy Jenkins, is the main editor and staff writer. She isn't always factual, though. In fact, Kathy Jenkins has written some pretty nasty (untrue!) stuff about Manny and me.

"I was a lifeguard at the community pool," Petula says. "That's how I got this perfect tan!"

She holds out her arm so all of us can inspect what must be Petula's perfect tan.

"One time, while on the job, I jumped in after a dog leaped off the diving board!" Petula continues. "On second thought, maybe that was Peter!"

Everyone at the table laughs. Peter *was* a bit obnoxious at Petula's pool party this summer. He kept doing these MONSTER CANNON-BALLS off the diving board and splashing everyone. The first time it was kinda funny, but by the fourth time it was, well, annoying.

"Ha-ha, very funny," Peter says. "But if you can't tell the difference between me and a dog—"

"Oh, I can tell," Petula says. "A dog spills less food on the floor when he eats!"

Again, everyone laughs.

"How about you, Clayton?" I ask. "What'd you do?

Clayton Harris is president of the Fillmore Middle School Inventors Club, a club I started. I was happy to hand it over to Clayton, though. Being a kid inventor and keeping up with schoolwork is hard—and it looks like it's going to get a lot harder.

"Well, Billy, I'm glad you asked," Clayton replies. "I started work on ten new inventions, which I hope to complete with the help of my fellow inventors club members."

"Ten! Wow!" I say, a little jealous that Clayton had a way more productive summer than I did.

"Yep, including a CHOCOLATE MILK LOCATOR, a HOMEWORK ORGANIZER, and an AUTOMATIC TABLE CLEARER," Clayton explains.

A Homework Organizer? That invention

sounds like something I could use right now! Clayton is a really smart inventor.

As I eat my peanut-butter-and-jelly-stuffed pickles, I glance around at the food on everyone's tray. Cafeteria food is notoriously bad no matter what school you go to (one of the reasons I like to bring to my own lunch every day—even if Dad does make it), but the stuff on everyone's plates today looks downright nasty.

Just as I'm about to ask what the weird-looking food is, Petula blurts out proudly: "You know, my aunt is the new director of Cafeteria Services."

So she's the one responsible for serving up a plate full of something that looks like it just crawled out from under a rock. And now that Petula says it, I remember her mentioning it at her pool party. The food there was super . . . um, "creative"—detox health shakes, creamy kale salad, and some seriously mysterious mystery meat!

And now this!

"My aunt went to Fillmore when she was

12

growing up," Petula continues. "She is *sooooo* cool! Look at what she did here. She used food coloring to make the chicken fingers match our school colors! How awesome is that?"

Wait. Hold up. CHICKEN FINGERS? Those gross green hunks of twisted stuff are supposed to be CHICKEN FINGERS?!

I don't know about your school, but at my school chicken fingers are the best cafeteria food we have. Why would anyone ruin Chicken Fingers Day? Everyone knows Chicken Fingers Day is the best day of the month! And these chicken fingers, they look, well, like . . . *fingers*.

Everyone has a pile of them on their trays, but as I eat my own lunch I notice that Petula is the only one actually eating them. The rest of my friends are working hard to eat the rest of the stuff on their plates—slowly sipping on cartons of milk, using their plastic spork to eat purple sorbet. I don't blame them.

But not Petula. Whether she actually likes the way they taste or she's eating them out of loyalty to her aunt, she devours one chicken finger after another, until at last lunch is over.

BRIIIIIIING!

The bell rings and we all get up from the table.

"This was fun!" says Peter. "Wanna meet for ice cream after school?"

I think about all the homework I have on day one of the eighth grade. Then I think about the chocolate mint marshmallow cookie-dough swirl sundae I could be eating instead. Magically, all thoughts about my homework DISAPPEAR.

"Sure," I say. "I'm in!"

Manny nods, followed by the rest of the gang. Even Petula, who seems to have survived her aunt's chicken fingers, agrees.

The rest of the day goes by smoothly, though I wonder if all the teachers got together and said, "Let's pull a practical joke on the kids and *all* give them a ton of homework on the first day!"

When the last bell of the day rings, I hop on my bike and head toward Jansen's Ice-Cream

Shop, which is on my way home anyway. My friends and I squeeze in around a not-quite-big-enough table in the middle of the restaurant. I can barely see Manny over my triple scoop sundae of chocolate mint marshmallow cookie-dough swirl.

We all start talking excitedly—this time about the new movie *Galaxy Battles: Episode Nine*, which is coming out this week. Celebrity actress Gemma Weston is starring in it, but even though we're kind of friends, she won't give away any secrets.

"I heard someone is going to lose a hand in the new movie," Allison says, then cheerfully licks her strawberry shortcake ice cream.

"*A* hand? No way. I think someone will lose *two* hands," says Peter. He dives into his cotton-candy scoop with animal-cracker crumbles.

We all jump right in. Everyone has their own theories.

Me? I don't really care. I'm just having a good time.

I shove another spoonful of delicious, chocolate-y ice cream into my mouth and notice that although I'm having a lot of fun, something is a LITTLE STRANGE here. I look around the table and realize what's strange is . . . Petula.

Petula has a scoop of vanilla ice cream with rainbow sprinkles in front of her, but she hasn't eaten a single bite. In fact, she looks a little green. And not in the "pistachio-ice-cream green" kind of way.

And Petula, who is one of the chattiest people I know (and that's a fact—I once timed her talking nonstop for a SOLID HOUR), has not said a single word.

"Are you okay, Petula?" I ask, wiping brown-and-white dribble from my chin.

"Hur," Petula grunts.

That's weird.

"How's your ice cream, Petula?" I ask.

"Hur." Another grunt.

The group resumes talking for an hour, until it's time to head home. As everyone gathers their stuff, I pull Manny aside.

"Does Petula seem a little, I don't know, STRANGE?" I whisper to him.

Manny shrugs.

"She was fine at lunch—I'm sure everything is okay," he says. "She might just be stressed because of all of the homework. I know I am."

Manny? Stressed?

Okay, now I KNOW eighth grade is going to be hard.

Chapter Two

Emily Sure—Reporter

WHEN I aRRIVE HOME, MY DOG, PHILO, COMES
trotting toward me. His tail wags, his tongue
flops, and he pants excitedly.

"No, boy, we're not going to work today," I
explain, wishing not for the first time that the
Cat-Dog Translator I invented was around.

See, my typical routine is to come home
from school, pick up Philo, then head over to
World Headquarters of Sure Things, Inc. (which
is conveniently located in Manny's garage).
Philo is very used to spending his afternoons
at the office with Manny and me, but since I

have a lot of homework to do, Manny and
I decided it's best if we work from home
this afternoon.

Once Philo gets the idea that we're stay-
ing put, he trots over to his doggy bed, circles
around twice, then hunkers down, sighing as
he wraps his tail around his back legs.

And speaking of HUNKERING DOWN . . .
I head up to my room to begin sorting through
the mountain of homework I have. Maybe if

I'm lucky I'll finish all this homework before I graduate!

Halfway up the stairs I run into Emily. She's in a great mood, something that always puts me a little on guard. Don't get me wrong, I'm happy my sister is happy, but the last time I saw her smiling this much, she thought we were moving to Italy.

"I cannot believe how great sophomore year is going to be!" Emily squeals.

Okay, I guess that's good.

"As a sophomore, I can take electives," Emily explains, even though I didn't ask her anything. "I get to choose from a whole bunch of classes, not just the usual stuff. Guess what I picked?"

I didn't know there was going to be a quiz.

"Um," I say, at the same time as she squeals, "JOURNALISM!"

"That's right, Billy, your beautiful, talented older sister is going to be a *journalist*. And guess who my teacher is!"

I stare blankly at her.

"Kathy Jenkins!"

Kathy Jenkins? Samantha's mom Kathy Jenkins, who writes all the bad stuff about Manny and me? I mean, I guess she's not a bad writer . . . but I really don't want my sister learning how to make things up!

"You're kidding, right?" I say, stunned. Just what I need . . . my sister making up things about me, right here in my very own home!

"For your information, Billy, Kathy Jenkins is a TOP-NOTCH PROFESSIONAL," Emily says.

She turns, heads into her room, and shuts the door.

I guess I have to add "be careful of what you say around Emily" to my homework list!

I settle down at my desk and sort through my assignments. I'm about halfway done when I'm saved by the bell—or, more accurately, saved by my mom.

"Billy!" she shouts from downstairs. "Dinner's ready! Pizza!"

Pizza? Yes! Just as I'm dreaming about a

slice of ULTRA-CHEESY pepperoni pizza, I stop dead in my tracks. The kitchen doesn't smell like delicious takeout pizza. It smells like . . .

"DONUT-KALE-TROUT PIZZA!" Dad says gleefully. "I know how much you kids like pizza. Here's my new special recipe!"

I slow my pace a bit, hoping that the salt shaker is fully loaded with GROSS-TO-GOOD POWDER, which does exactly what it sounds like it does. I don't know about your taste in pizza toppings, but for me, this latest "Dad recipe" sounds like it's going to need LOTS and LOTS of the stuff.

The next morning at school I hurry down the hall. As I'm rushing in, I see Petula walking toward me.

But something is still very wrong with her. Petula is a really good athlete. She's just about the best swimmer I know, captain of the Fillmore swim team, and a certified lifeguard. Most of the trophies in the FILLMORE

HALL OF FAME are there because of her. But today she walks slowly down the hall, stiff legged, like she can hardly bend her knees. Her arms extend in front of her and she shuffles from side to side. She doesn't have the usual smoothness in her movement and bounce in her step.

Hmm. Maybe she has an injury that she hasn't told anyone about? Maybe that's why she's being so quiet—she doesn't want to talk about it.

"Hey, Petula, how are you feeling today?" I ask when I'm just a few feet away.

"GURURRR," she grunts, staring straight ahead, walking right past me.

Hmm. This kinda reminds me of someone—Emily. Emily just finished going through a phase in which she didn't speak for days, just grunted and groaned.

As it turned out, Emily was being quiet because she had recently gotten braces, and for some reason she didn't want anyone to see.

I wonder if Petula got braces too.

I push thoughts about Petula aside and finish up my first few classes of day two of eighth grade. It's even busier than day one—and I get EVEN MORE homework!

Finally, lunchtime rolls around.

I meet my friends at the long table in the cafeteria and pull out my two slices of leftover pizza. A piece of donut with chocolate frosting crumbles to the floor.

"Interesting toppings," Manny says, opening up his peanut butter and banana sandwich. A piece of the trout on the left side of my pizza wiggles off.

"Mhm," I say through the first mouthful.

One by one, the rest of our friends return from the lunch line. They each carry a tray full of today's lunch special—green shepherd's pie. Once again the new cafeteria director has tried to match the Fillmore Middle School colors. And in truth, she's done a pretty good job at getting the green *just right*—not that it makes the round creepy-looking thing on everyone's tray look any more appealing!

I decide to ignore it.

"Have you heard the latest?" Clayton asks, in between bites of his shepherd's pie. "Principal Gilamon dyed his hair PURPLE!"

"Really?" I ask. "Why would he do that?"

But before anyone can answer, the bell rings. As I get up from the table I realize that

Peter MacHale, who might rival Petula in talkativeness, hasn't said a single word. Typically, Peter can't wait to gossip about the latest news, and Principal Gilamon dyeing his hair purple? *Definitely* news.

But today . . . nothing.

"Hey, Peter, what do you think about Principal Gilamon's new hair? It's *interesting*, right?" I ask, egging him on.

"Hurrrr," Peter groans.

He stands up slowly and walks away from the table with that same stiff-legged walk that Petula now has.

Normally, Peter would just go on and on about something like Principal Gilamon's purple hair. If you want to know what's going on with anyone at school, Peter is the go-to guy. But today he's quiet, just like Petula.

As the rest of my friends get up from the cafeteria table, I notice that all of them—with the exception of Manny—are also quiet. No one says "see ya," or "text ya," or "talk to ya later," or any of the other usual things we say to each other when lunch is over.

What's going on with them? Did EVERYONE *I know get braces all at the same time?*

It's one thing to have an older sister who always seems to be into some bizarre new thing, but to have all your friends suddenly get into the same "thing" at the same time—well, that is just plain weird.

Chapter Three

Manny's Plan

EVEN THOUGH I HAVE A TON OF HOMEWORK AGAIN, I decide to visit the office after school. There's simply no way around it. I need to talk to Manny about what's going on with all our friends.

I stop at home and drop off all of my books. Then I hop on my bike and pedal away, with Philo keeping pace beside me.

Manny greets me at the office.

"Manny, I have something to ask you," I say. "Have you noticed that our friends are . . . acting odd lately?"

I don't know how else to put it.

"Hmm," Manny says. He scratches his chin. "I ran into Samantha Jenkins on my way home from school. I guess it was a little strange. She didn't say a word."

I nod.

"And was she moving really slow—like, stiff legged?"

Manny ponders this again.

"You know what, partner, I think you're on to something," he says, as casually and calmly as only Manny can. "Yesterday morning Petula was her usual chatty self. Then after lunch she—"

Manny pauses. I can almost see the lightbulb go on above his head!

"Lunch!" he repeats.

"Lunch?" I ask.

Then I feel the lightbulb go on above *my* head.

"Lunch!! What if all this is because of the new school lunches? What if it's making everyone sick?"

"You may be right," Manny says. "Since Petula's aunt took over as director of Cafeteria Services, everything they're serving looks super gross."

"I haven't taken a single bite of it," I point out. "And neither have you. We've both been bringing lunch from home. And we're the only ones who are fine."

Manny thinks for a moment. I know better than to interrupt the silence.

"There's only one way we can find out what's going on," he finally says. He almost sounds . . . brave? "One of us is going to have to eat the school lunch and see what happens."

I gulp. Manny's right, of course—that is the scientific method, after all. But *eat* that gross food, and turn into a grunting mess like our friends? I guess one of us has to. I take a deep breath.

"I'll do it," I say.

Manny shakes his head.

"No—I will," he says firmly. "Listen, partner, I appreciate you volunteering, but if this cafeteria food is what's making everyone act weird, I know that you can invent a cure. But if *you* eat it and something bad happens . . . let's just say that all the marketing plans in the world aren't going to help me cure everyone. I've got to be the volunteer."

As usual, Manny's argument is airtight. Reason #333 that I'm glad Manny is my best friend and business partner.

"Okay," I say. I do my best not to sound nervous, but I'm PRETTY NERVOUS. "I guess."

"It's settled, then," Manny says. "Tomorrow I'll eat the school lunch. Then we'll see what happens."

I hang around the office for a little while longer, but it's clear that it makes no sense for me to dive in to a new invention—I need to keep my mind (and my workbench) clear, in case our theory is correct and I need to invent an antidote of sorts. I head home.

On the way to my room after dinner, Emily catches me on the stairs. She has a pencil behind her ear. She kind of looks like Dad when he has a paintbrush behind his ear. Oh yeah, Dad's an artist. His art is very, um, creative. But why does my sister have a pencil behind her ear?

Is this her new thing? I wonder. (My sister has new "things" all the time. Sometimes she picks up totally new "things"—like only speaking with an English accent or wearing some pretty funky hats—for a brief amount of time. She then drops them as quickly as they come.) *If it is, it's pretty tame.*

Before I can ask her about it, she snatches the pencil from behind her ear and pulls a small notebook from her pocket.

Yikes, not so tame.

"So, Billy Sure, is anything interesting going on at Fillmore Middle School?" she asks, flashing a GREAT BIG SMILE. "I'm journalist Emily Sure and I need to know the scoop."

I know my sister well enough to know when her smile is fake. And this is one of the fakest smiles I've ever seen. Maybe I would have told

her about the weird stuff going on at Fillmore
once upon a time, but now that Kathy Jenkins
is her teacher, Emily is the last person I'm
going to talk about it with.

"Good night, Em," I say, trying to slip past
her.

No luck. She stands in the middle of the
stairs, blocking my way.

"Okay, okay, not Fillmore Middle School,"
she says, tapping her pencil on the notebook.

"Can you tell me anything about what's going on at Sure Things, Inc.? How is your latest invention, the CANDY TOOTHBRUSH selling? How is Manny feeling? *Anything?!*"

No scientific method here needed. Emily is *definitely* being taught by Kathy Jenkins.

"See ya, Em," I say, faking left, then spinning right and slipping past her up the stairs. "I really have a lot of homework to finish. Why don't you interview Dad, see how his newest art project is going?"

Without waiting for an answer, I head to my room. Jada and I text a bit. Apparently while I was at school and my friends acted weird, she hung out with her neighbor, Kevin. She sends me a picture of them at the park. As I doze off to sleep, I feel a little jealous of Kevin.

The next day in the cafeteria, I wait for Manny, nervous about what's going to happen.

"Hey, Billy!" I hear Manny say. When I turn around, we're no longer in the cafeteria.

Instead, we are inside an AMUSEMENT PARK FUNHOUSE!

I see that Manny is decked out in heavy armor—though by "armor" I mean a spaghetti pot for a helmet and a lunch tray as a shield. I glance down and see that I'm also dressed the same way.

None of our friends are in sight. Kevin is there, though. He laughs at me.

"What's going on, Manny?" I ask.

But before I can answer, a giant slab of green meat with arms and legs *and* eyes appears! It starts chasing us. We run around and tumble through a TRAP DOOR.

Down we go, skidding along a twisting, turning playground slide in the dark.

I see something up ahead.

"Look out, Manny!" I cry, spotting a flurry of knives, forks, napkins, and small packets of ketchup and mustard zooming toward us!

We both press our backs into the slide and watch the silverware and condiments whiz past our heads. *Phew,* I think. *That was close.*

We rush toward something at the end of the slide.

"What is T̲H̲A̲T̲?!" I shout.

SPLOOOCH!

We both land in a pile soft pile of . . . of . . . something. . . .

"What is this stuff?" I ask Manny, pulling globs of greenish-brown gunk out of my hair.

"Looks like moldy hot dogs and buns to me," Manny says.

"That is correct," says a voice. It's one of the hot dogs! "You have eaten us for your whole life. Now it's time for us to eat *you!*"

We get up and start running down a dark hallway. I look back over my shoulder and see about a HUNDRED moldy hot dogs chasing us.

At the end of the hallway we come to a door with a flickering sign. It reads: THIS WAY OUT—IF YOU DARE!

"No other choice!" Manny shouts, as if he can read my mind. "Let's go!"

I yank open the door and run through—then find myself FACE TO FACE with the entire Fillmore Middle School cafeteria staff, led by Petula's aunt.

Only they don't look like the Fillmore Middle School cafeteria staff. They look like monsters! Droopy, terrifying monsters. Each one clutches a cooking utensil and holds it up in a menacing fashion.

"Aaaaurghhhh," the lunch staff says in unison, waving spatulas, egg beaters, and can openers at us. Kevin has joined them and has the scariest spatula of all. I've never seen a spatula look so . . . well, dangerous, before.

And that's when I wake up, breathing hard.

I look at the clock. It's time to get up and go to school.

Phew. At least that was only a dream, I think.

But what's going to happen to Manny in the cafeteria today?!

Chapter Four

Figuring It Out

THE NEXT DAY MY PROBLEMS START THE MINUTE I
step into the Fillmore Middle School building.
First of all, Jada doesn't respond to my text
about *Sandbox XXL*, and I'm nervous she would
rather play the game with Kevin now. Second,
as I walk down the hall, I see something EVEN
MORE HAUNTING than the crazy dream I
had last night.

It's no longer just the members of my little
group of friends that are acting strange. It seems
that EVERY KID in the school has changed!
They're all walking in that stiff-legged fashion,

with their arms extended out in front of them. And—this might just be my imagination, but they all look a little . . . *green*.

The other thing that's so eerie is that the halls are quiet. Normally, they are buzzing

with a million conversations as kids hurry from class to class. But today the only sounds are soft groans. "Arrrrrrrghhhhh."

None of the kids even notice I'm there.

Lunchtime finally arrives. I feel myself getting more and more anxious the closer I get to the cafeteria. I walk in and see that Manny is already there, sitting at a long table with our friends. Only Manny looks like his normal self . . . for now, anyway. The other kids stare intensely at their trays.

I sit down and pull out my sandwich that Dad made—watermelon, halibut, and goat cheese between two waffles—when I see that Manny has a big plate of gross-looking green lunch meat piled up in front of him. I know it's part of the plan, but it makes me feel sick anyway.

"Well, partner, it's time for our LITTLE EXPERIMENT," Manny says, poking at the mysterious meat on his plate with a fork. "At least we'll know what's going on. If this is what's making everyone sick, I KNOW you'll be able to invent the cure. I have complete confidence in you."

I gulp. Manny kind of sounds like he's giving a farewell speech at the end of a monster movie.

"Here we go. Three . . . two . . . one."

I hold my breath. Manny lifts up his fork piled with the mysterious lunch meat on it. It almost looks like a green radioactive sponge. He takes a whiff of it.

"Smells like chicken," Manny says, smiling. Then he takes a big bite.

I brace myself. Any moment now, Manny is going to start groaning . . .

"How was it?" I ask, fearing the worst.

"Well, it definitely doesn't *taste* good," Manny says.

What?! Manny! He's still here! How—?

"But I don't think it did anything weird to me," he finishes.

Manny takes another bite. Nothing. Then another. Nope. Still no change.

I exhale and relax a bit. Okay, I think.

The good news is that Manny is okay. The bad news—we still don't know what's causing everyone to turn green and act strange.

I finish my sandwich and get up to get some more juice. When I get back to the table, a new idea strikes me.

"You know, Manny, Petula *is* the president of the FILLMORE DRAMA CLUB," I say, feeling weird that I'm speaking about Petula in front of her. Something tells me she hasn't noticed, though. A big glob of drool splatters down from Petula's chin. "Maybe she's got everyone rehearsing for a drama club performance? Some sort of flash mob? It would be a pretty cool stunt idea, don't you think?"

Manny says nothing. He continues to shove lunch meat into his mouth.

"Manny?" I ask again. "Do you think that's possible?" It's weird. Manny doesn't usually ignore me.

Again, Manny doesn't respond.

"Manny?" I ask. "Manny, did you hear me?"

No response.

"Manny!" I say loudly.

Manny stops eating. He looks at me and grunts. There's drool dripping down from his chin.

"URRRGHHH," he says. Then he goes back to eating.

And that's when I see it.

Manny has turned green!

We were right. It *is* the lunch meat that's changing everyone into . . . into . . .

Oh no. I look over at Manny again. He's green, he's groaning, and he's shoveling food into his mouth.

Wait a minute! Manny looks like he did that time the two of us were on the set of the movie *Alien Zombie Attack!* We were covered in makeup. We were playing zombies!

I feel my heart start to pound. That's it! ZOMBIES. The kids at Fillmore Middle School are turning into zombies. But not movie zombies. *Real* zombies. Everyone is a REAL ZOMBIE!

But how? And why? Does Petula's aunt know?

Trying to stay focused, I stab a piece of the lunch meat with a fork and slip it into the resealable plastic bag my sandwich came in. Now that we know this food is the problem, I'll need to do some studies. I hurry from the cafeteria, my mind racing.

What's going to happen to Sure Things, Inc. if I can't invent a cure? What's going to happen to the school? My friends? Manny?

Should I tell Dr. and Mr. Reyes about what happened to Manny? I mean, they're certainly going to notice that something is up when they ask their son, "How was school today?" and all he says is, "Urrrhhh. . . ."

And what about everyone else at Fillmore Middle School? What will the teachers say?

The school nurse? The janitors? Principal Gilamon?

Principal Gilamon? PRINCIPAL GILAMON! That's it. I have to tell Principal Gilamon. He's got to know that there is a major emergency going on in his school. He's got to know that the school lunch is turning all the students into zombies!

I've got to hurry. I've got to see him before anyone else turns into a zombie.

I race through the halls, ducking past the shuffling zombie students of Fillmore Middle School. Thankfully, it's not that hard. They're not exactly fast.

I walk into the front office and see Mr. Hairston, Principal Gilamon's always-grumpy administrative assistant. His head is tilted down toward his desk. He looks like he's filling out some forms.

"Mr. Hairston, I need to see Principal Gilamon right this second," I say, still trying to catch my breath. "This is a TRUE, GENUINE, ONE HUNDRED PERCENT

EMERGENCY. I wouldn't burst in here like this unless it was really, really serious!"

Mr. Hairston shrugs in disapproval. I've seen him like this before. He gets stuck on tiny details. For example, I don't have an appointment, and he doesn't like that. Although he's been impatient and fussy before, he's never ignored me.

"Mr. Hairston, this is very important. The whole school has turned into—"

Mr. Hairston finally looks up. I gasp. I can see why he's been ignoring me now.

HIS FACE IS GREEN!

"Hrrruggh!" he groans.

Oh no! Mr. Hairston is a zombie!

Chapter Five

Billy Sure . . . Not a Zombie!

I FEEL MY HANDS GET CLAMMY AS I STARE AT THE door to Principal Gilamon's office. I walk in and find him at his desk, intensely concentrating, writing.

Phew! At least that's pretty normal, I think. *A middle school principal writing. Yup, pretty normal.*

The only thing ABNORMAL about this picture is that Principal Gilamon's hair is now purple. Not only is it purple, it's spiked up into a Mohawk. Not that there's anything wrong with Mohawks, of course—it's just kind of funny to see your school principal sporting one. If today

were a normal day, I'd be recommending that Emily get the scoop on this for her journalism class, but today is not a normal day. Today I need Principal Gilamon's help, and I need it STAT.

"Principal Gilamon, I think something is horribly wrong in the school cafeteria," I say quickly. I know I should slow down and enunciate, but I can't help it. "The lunch meat our new director of Cafeteria Services is serving—well, it's making everyone sick!"

Best not to start off with the whole zombie thing. It would probably sound pretty crazy.

"So, um, everyone is getting sick and I'm really worried and Manny and I went to test the lunch meat and . . . and . . . "

And that's when I notice that Principal Gilamon hasn't said a word. He hasn't looked up from his papers. He hasn't even acknowledged that I'm here.

Oh no. . . .

"Principal Gilamon?"

It's my worst fear.

Principal Gilamon has become a zombie too! Mayday. Mayday. This is NOT a dream!

I race from the office, run past Mr. Hairston, and dash out into the hall. The crowd of zombie students seems to have grown. I push my way past them. They don't seem to notice.

I've *got* to find someone to help me. I've got to get to the bottom of this. But also, I can't solve this all by myself. If only Manny hadn't eaten that lunch meat!

As if to make matters worse, Jada *finally* answers my text. It's been three hours. She's never taken this long before. She says she got burgers with—you guessed it—Kevin. I feel a pit in my stomach. What makes Kevin so important?

I'm thinking about Kevin and zombies in my next scheduled class, English. Ms. Nading is the teacher. Maybe she'll be able to help me.

I slip into her classroom and take my seat. Looking around, I see that every student in the class is green. The students sit, swaying back and forth, MOANING and GROANING in unison.

It sounds to me, for the first time, like the kids are actually trying to say something. Like they are trying to form words, not just grunts.

"Louuukkkkk maaaayyyt!" they seem to say at the same time.

What does that mean? What are they trying to say?

As I ponder this, Ms. Nading walks into the room.

And she's green too! She walks, stiff legged to a laptop which is connected to a projector. She clicks on a movie.

A movie? In English class? On the second day of school? I mean, I guess a zombie teacher can't really do much else, but . . . this is *English* class, and it's a movie about—you guessed it—zombies!

I sit through the movie, listening to my classmates groan. I wish I could text Jada about all of this, but she's probably off eating burgers with Kevin.

"Luuncckkkkk maeaaayyt!" my classmates yelp.

When the bell rings, I bolt from the classroom.

My next class is science. Once again, every kid in the class is a zombie. Once again, they groan that same, weird language in unison.

And again, the teacher, Ms. Soo, is also a zombie. And she also puts on a movie.

Don't get me wrong, I generally like watching movies in class. I'm sure you know the feeling—getting into class on a day when you feel like it's going to be hard, but then, surprise! There's a screen up. It usually means a pretty easy class. But now, today, with what's going on, I would really love someone to talk to, someone to help me figure out what to do!

The movie ends, the bell rings, and I go out into the hall . . . where it looks like every kid in the school has gathered.

Something is different about these kids, though. As soon as I step into the hall, they all turn and look right at me. Before, they acted like they didn't even see me. Now they all march toward me, arms extended!

It looks like they're coming after me. But what do they want?!

"LUUUUNCH MEEEEEAT!" the whole mob says at once.

Did they just say "lunch meat"?

"Luuuunch meeeeeat!" the mob says again.

They come closer, stiff legged and arms outstretched.

"Luuuunch meeeeeat!"

Is this a dream? Maybe it's a dream. I grab hold of my arm and pinch it *really hard* just in case, but all it does is make me say "ow."

Nope. Definitely not a dream.

I have to get out of the school. I have to find help somewhere else.

But how?!

The mob blocks the entire hallway leading to the front door of the school. There's no way I can slip past them. I'm TRAPPED!

Chapter Six

Help On the Way

WITH THE WAY TO THE FRONT DOOR BLOCKED BY lunch meat-craving zombie students, I turn and run down the hall in the opposite direction through a back door. It's a good choice. I end up right in the parking lot and spot my bike—but a zombie-kid is on it. "Go away!" I screech, and grab my bike quickly away from him. I've got to get home and save the day!

Before I even realize it, I'm pedaling as hard as I ever have, going faster than I've ever gone on a bike. My heart is racing. It seems that my speeding mind has made my feet speed up too.

Calm down, Billy. Panicking will not help. Think. Think!

I force my feet to slow down. Somehow, that helps my mind clear a bit as well. I know what I have to do. I have to find someone else who has not been turned into a lunch meat-craving zombie to help me. I can't do this alone. But who can help me? Everyone at my school seems to be affected.

Well, there are people who DON'T *go to your school,* I think, and then it dawns on me. JADA PARIKH AND NAT DEFINITE! Their school year hasn't started yet. And they are both really smart!

As I pull into my driveway, I jump off my bike and take out my phone. I set up a group text to Jada and Nat. Surely, Jada can't ignore this one . . . no matter HOW cool Kevin is. . . .

Major emergency! No joke. Meet me at HQ in an hour? Manny can explain better than me.

You know what they say. *"One zombie is worth a thousand words."*

Okay, maybe they don't really say that.

I say an hour because Manny should be home by then. Then I feed Philo and grab myself a snack—I'm not hungry, but I've got to make sure I'm still eating.

As I pedal my way toward the World Headquarters of Sure Things, Inc. (also known as HQ), I wonder how Philo is going to react to ZOMBIE MANNY. The poor dog was confused enough when Manny and I traded work stations this summer, what's he going to do when he sees zombie Manny?

I pull up to HQ. Jada and Nat are waiting outside.

"Are you okay?" Jada asks. Is it bad how happy I am to see her?

I guess . . . well, I guess I look a little green, but for a totally different reason! I'm nervous! At least having Jada around makes me feel more comfortable now.

"I'm fine," I say. "But I'm just about the

only one at Fillmore Middle School who is."

"You said you had a MAJOR EMER-GENCY," says Nat. "What's going on, Billy?"

"I gotta show you," I reply. "Come on, let's go in, but be prepared for a bit of a shock."

Nat, Jada, and I enter the World Headquarters. Manny is sitting at his desk. His back is to us. From behind, he looks perfectly normal.

"Hi, Manny," says Nat. "Nice to see you." She blushes.

Nat used to have a big crush on Manny. Okay, I get the feeling she still does.

"Urrgg . . . ," Manny groans.

"Manny?" Nat says, walking around to the front of his desk.

Jada and I join her. That's when Jada and Nat see that Manny has turned green! He stares at his computer screen, pointing vaguely every few seconds.

Philo walks slowly over to Manny and sniffs him. He whines, then quickly heads back to his doggy bed, where he buries his head under his paws.

"Something is very wrong!" Nat says. "We have to do something. Billy, what is this all about? And more importantly, what can we do about it?"

I quickly fill them in on what's been going on at Fillmore Middle School.

"This reminds me of an epidemic straight out of *Sandbox XXL*," Jada says. "Level eighty-four, extended discontinued Japanese edition. Kevin and I had to help each other on this one. We need to invent a cure. And who better than you two to do that?" She looks at Nat and me.

"GOOD THINKING," says Nat. "Billy, do you have a sample of the mysterious lunch meat for us to analyze?"

Now I'm really glad that I thought to take that piece of lunch meat from the cafeteria.

"I have one right here," I say, opening up my backpack and pulling out the plastic sandwich bag. I hand it to Nat, who sits at my workbench.

"Be careful," I say.

"I'm a professional," she replies.

Nat slips on protective yellow goggles, gloves, and stretches a mask across her mouth. She looks a **LITTLE SILLY**! She opens the bag.

As soon as Nat takes the sample meat out of the bag, Manny sniffs the air a couple of times, turns his head, and starts to stand up.

"Luuuunch meeeeeat!" he growls.

"Nat, you've got to work fast!" I cry. "Or Manny will end up eating our only sample, and we can't leave the office—it's the only safe place for these tests!"

"Luuuunch meeeeeat!" he groans again, stumbling toward Nat.

Nat works furiously, mixing ingredients and taking tests. She is about to soak the lunch meat in her bubbling chemical concoction when Manny reaches for the bench.

"Faster, Nat, faster!" I shout.

"I'm a professional, not a magician!" Nat cries.

Manny reaches out to grab the sample from Nat's hand. She quickly slips the meat back into the bag and reseals it.

Manny stops, sniffs a few times and looks around. With the scent of the lunch meat no longer in the room, Manny shuffles back to his desk.

Nat, Jada, and I huddle around my workbench. For a brief second, Jada's hand touches mine. A shiver goes up my spine. Okay, I kind of like Jada. More than "kind of."

"I didn't have long to analyze that sample, but I do have a theory," Nat says.

"I don't think this is lunch meat at all," she continues. "I think that this—this—this *stuff*, is a NEW INVENTION specifically designed to turn people into zombies!"

A new invention?!

We're dealing with *another inventor* here?

"But *why?*" I yelp. "It doesn't make any sense. Petula's aunt is the one who served this in the cafeteria. Is she behind this? Why would she want to turn everyone into zombies?"

"That's the MILLION DOLLAR QUESTION, isn't it?" says Jada.

"I'll need to do a deeper analysis of this sample," says Nat. "That might give us some clues about why Petula's aunt would do this. But, obviously, I can't do it here. Not with . . . not with Manny this way."

Nat really likes Manny, and I can tell that seeing him this way is very upsetting to her.

"Why don't I try working on this in my own lab?" she suggests.

"Good idea," I say.

"I'll get to work on it right away," says Nat. "If I come up with anything, I'll text you tonight."

"Thanks, guys," I say, and the four of us (Philo included) head for the door.

I might be imagining it, but it kind of looks like Jada is sad to see me go.

Just as I'm about to leave, I turn around and look at zombie Manny. "I miss you, partner," I tell him. "We're going to fix this. I promise."

But as I bike home with Philo by my side, I'm not so sure.

Can we fix this? Or is this a food fight Sure Things, Inc. can't win?

There's something going on here. Something deeper than meets the eye. But how can I dig deeper to uncover unknown information? I'm an inventor, not a spy!

Wait a minute . . . a SPY!

That's it! Last year, I found out my mom is a spy. Yup, a real spy, with real missions and cool gadgets. I may not be a spy, but Mom certainly is! Maybe Mom can help me solve this puzzle once and for all!

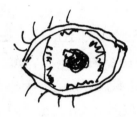

Chapter Seven

On the Case

I BURST INTO THE HOUSE. IF ANYONE CAN GET TO the bottom of this, it's Mom. Mom is a *real* spy who works for the government. She can probably solve a small problem like her son's entire middle school turning into lunch meat-craving zombies in a FLASH.

But on my way up the stairs to Mom's office, I'm ambushed by Emily. She takes her pencil out from behind her ear and holds up a notepad.

"Billy Sure!" Emily shouts, as if she is surprised to see me here in my own house. "Billy

Sure, can you give me the scoop? Any interesting stories? Breaking news? Anything going on
I should know about?"

She's ready to pounce on my every word.

I laugh. It's not because I'm trying to make fun of Emily, or because I think she won't make a great reporter—let's be real, my sister's been annoying me for answers since day one. It's because at this exact moment she looks so much like Kathy Jenkins, it's uncanny!

"So, what's going on?"

Emily is persistent, I'll give her that.

Hmm . . . a crazy thought HITS me. Emily *is* pretty good at digging deep, researching, and finding hidden information. Maybe she can help me uncover the truth of this story. In fact, maybe I won't even need to bother Mom with this at all! Emily is *technically* Sure Things, Inc.'s Very Official Hollywood Coordinator anyway, so we can keep this as a Sure Things, Inc. and Definite Devices operative team.

"Okay, Em, I have a story for you," I say. "And it's not just a gossipy, plain ol' 'gotcha!' type story. It's a real mystery, and a threat to the very existence of Fillmore Middle School!"

Emily rolls her eyes at me.

"Are you making fun of me?" she asks. "Do

you think I'm not smart enough to be taken seriously as a reporter?"

"No. This is real. And I need your help," I say.

"Okay then," Emily sighs. I can tell she doesn't really believe me. "SPILL."

"What if I told you that there is a new director of Cafeteria Services at Fillmore Middle School?"

Emily raises an eyebrow.

"Riveting," she says coldly. "I can see the headline now. Breaking news—'New Director, Same Bad Food.' I need a little something more to work with, Billy. Yawn."

"Well," I say, "what if I told you that the new director is serving some REALLY WEIRD lunch meat?"

"Double yawn."

"Okay," I smile now. I may be worried, but I'll never miss an opportunity to tease my older sister. "What if I told you that the weird lunch meat is turning all the kids at Fillmore Middle School into zombies?"

Emily stops writing.

She glares at me.

"'INVENTOR BILLY SURE REALLY IS BANANAS, AND REPORTER EMILY SURE HAS THE SCOOP,'" she pretends to read the headline aloud.

"No, really. They are zombies, Em. Students, teachers, even Principal Gilamon have turned into zombies!"

Emily gets quiet for a moment. She taps her pencil on her notepad.

"Why aren't you working with Manny on this?" she asks suspiciously.

"Because Manny is a zombie too!" I admit.

Her eyes open wide. For the first time I think she believes me. She knows I wouldn't lie about Manny.

"Okay, okay, this is good, really," she says, writing as fast as she can. "I mean, it's bad, I get that, but . . . this is an *excellent* story, Billy! It might even get me on the high school paper! Or published on *Right Next Door*! Okay, let's get to work."

Emily and I sit at the kitchen table and

start to think through all the possible explanations for the zombie epidemic. But until we have more information, we're kind of stuck.

"How about this?" Emily says. "Tomorrow, during my investigative journalism time, I'll stop by your school and we'll see if we can figure this out. We'll have to start with the first step of journalism—going directly to the source, the director of Cafeteria Services. And then maybe we can solve this ZOMBIE EPIDEMIC!"

For someone about to dive head first into a zombie epidemic, Emily is a little too cheery.

"Did I just hear someone say something about investigating zombies?" says Mom, walking into the living room. "Are you guys in another movie?"

Hmm . . . well, I guess I've got to tell Mom now.

"No," I say. Then I quickly fill her in on the details of the VERY BIZARRE first few days of school.

"Well, this sounds like spy work to me,"

Mom says. "If I were identifying a suspect, I'd say the director of Cafeteria Services—Petula's aunt—is SUSPECT A. Everything changed after she took charge of the cafeteria food. We'll need to research her background, see if she has any connection to Fillmore, and use that information to see if we can figure out a motive. Once we know a motive, we'll know more. Or we can disprove that she's involved at all, and start a different approach."

That's my mom, the superspy!

"Things have been quiet on the whole 'saving the world' front at work, so I'm happy to help figure out what is really going on here."

"That's awesome, Mom!" I say.

Emily scribbles on her notepad, "WHEN NOTED SPY CAROL SURE JOINED THE INVESTIGATION, THINGS GOT REALLY INTERESTING."

"Are you writing the story before it's even over?" I ask.

"Just being prepared," Emily says, going back to her pad.

"Um, part of being a successful spy, Em, is

remaining anonymous," Mom points out. "So, I'm happy to help, but I think it would be best if you leave my name out of any article. Also, leave out Agent Paul's name too."

"Agent Paul, your spy partner?" I ask.

A few months ago I helped my mom on a mission to save Agent Paul. Oh, by the way, Agent Paul just happens to be an octopus.

"Yes, I have a feeling he'll come in HANDY on this case," Mom explains with a laugh.

Mom then brings out her briefcase and starts searching through it. She pulls out a tiny silver ring and a clear piece of plastic about the size of a credit card.

"What are those things?" I ask.

"Oh, just a few things the kids at Spy Academy came up with," Mom explains.

She picks up the small silver ring that looks like it would barely fit onto my pinky finger.

"If I squeeze this *just* right it becomes a pair of handcuffs," Mom says. "Xavier invented it."

Xavier was one of the kids I met when I spent some time at Spy Academy. He's a *really* smart inventor, though he kinda scared me at first.

Mom squeezes the ring and it pops open into a pair of pretty tough-looking handcuffs. Neat! Next she picks up the clear piece of plastic.

"Drew actually invented this one."

(Drew is another inventor at Spy Academy, though we didn't exactly get along.)

She presses the plastic between her palms and it expands, growing into a clear shield that surrounds her whole body.

"This shield is bullet proof, laser proof, and—"

"ZOMBIE PROOF?" Emily asks.

"I guess we'll find out," Mom says, smiling.

Drew is a good inventor, too, but he is also the nephew of Alistair Swiped, a rival inventor who used to steal ideas from Sure Things, Inc.

"Drew, huh?" I ask.

"Yes. Ever since Manny exposed his plan to put Sure Things, Inc. out of business, Drew has been a model student, a good spy, and a very clever inventor," Mom explains. Then she smiles and stops rummaging through her things. "Oh, here's what I'm looking for."

Mom pulls out a unique-looking contraption. It looks kind of like a phone with a small fishbowl full of water sitting on the top.

"Drew also came up with this one," Mom says. "It's my PAUL-O-PHONE! It translates English into Octopus, and the other way

around, so I can talk to Paul. Man, before this, I had *no idea* Agent Paul was so funny." Mom laughs, obviously remembering something. "I'll give him a call."

She presses three buttons on the Paul-O-Phone. The thing lights up and starts flashing, and the water in the tiny fishbowl starts bubbling.

"B-b-b-b-*hello?*" says a bubbly voice through the phone's speaker.

It sounds like Agent Paul is talking underwater, but I can actually understand what he's saying!

"Agent Paul, Agent Sure here. We've got a problem and I think you can help," Mom says. She quickly outlines our serious situation.

"Well, it's nice to *meat* you, Emily." Agent Paul laughs, when he learns that Emily is in the room. "This *definitely* sounds like I'm the right octopus for the job. I'm on my way!"

Chapter Eight

Team Sure on the Job

AGENT PAUL ARRIVES AT OUR HOUSE FIRST THING the next morning, and the four of us head to Fillmore Middle School. I hope today is going to be better. I wake up to a "good morning" text from Jada!

Normally, snooping around the building during a regular school day would be nearly impossible—even for professional spies like Mom and Agent Paul. There's just not much you can get past middle school kids. But today no one notices us.

We slip into the school and scoot past zombie

students. They wander aimlessly through the halls. Since we aren't carrying any lunch meat, they don't seem to notice us at all.

"Aren't there *any* real classes going on?" Mom asks. She's obviously concerned.

At that moment Mr. Jennings, Ms. Nading, Ms. Soo, and Ms. Ekuma all come walking down the hall. Their skin is green, and they shuffle, stiff legged toward us, muttering, "LUUUUNCH MEEEEEAT!"

"Not without teachers," I say, pointing. "And those are my teachers!"

Mom's face turns serious. I'm not sure that she had a true idea of how bad this situation really is.

We make our way down the hall, with Agent Paul's tank rolling along beside us.

"We've got to get our hands—and tentacles—on the school records," Mom says seriously. She kind of sounds like we're in an action film.

"Those would be in Principal Gilamon's office," I say. "This way!"

The closer we get to Principal Gilamon's office, the more nervous I get. I mean, why would you ever want to sneak into the principal's office? We pause outside his door, then slip in.

Mr. Hairston sits at his desk, head down, scribbling on one of his official appointment forms. His skin somehow looks even GREENER than it was yesterday! He definitely doesn't notice *three people and an octopus* sneaking past his desk.

Ah well. I'll have to worry about Mr. Hairston later. I open the door to Principal Gilamon's office. Principal Gilamon sits at his desk, mindlessly stamping the same form from yesterday over and over. He, too, doesn't notice the team sneaking past his desk. I wonder if he's been here all night, just stamping.

"This is even worse than I imagined," says Mom. I see her do a double take at Principal Gilamon's hair. "We've got to move fast!"

"The school records room is right there," I say, pointing to a door at the back of the principal's office. Back when I was Mr. Gilamon's GOLDEN BOY for being a famous kid inventor, he gave me a tour of his office.

"Well, what are we waiting for, then? Let's go search the school files!" says Emily.

"Wait," Mom says. "You can't just waltz into the records room and search the files, Em. I mean, *you* can't, as a student, but *I* can, as an official spy. So can Agent Paul."

"Um, Mom, have you noticed that we are in the MIDDLE OF A CRISIS here?" Emily asks.

"Rules are rules, Em," says Mom. "However, it would be okay for you and Billy to help us search through the files, *if* you get permission from Principal Gilamon. And I think that for time's sake it would be best if all four of us could search."

"I have an idea," says Emily. She switches on the voice recorder app on her phone. "Principal Gilamon, this is Emily Sure. I'm with my brother Billy and two OFFICIAL GOVERNMENT SPIES."

I can tell that Emily likes saying "official government spies"!

"We would all like your permission to read

the files on your staff at Fillmore Middle School."

Principal Gilamon grunts. We're not sure if he's reacting to what Emily just said or if he's just randomly grunting.

Emily continues, "We believe something mysterious is going on at the school, and we want to find out the truth. Is that all right with you?"

Principal Gilamon grunts again.

"Will you give us official authorization to search the school's files?"

Another grunt.

I can see that Emily is frustrated. She turns to me.

"Billy, if he won't give us permission to go through the Fillmore files, I don't know what to do! We need to help Mom find out more about this LOONY LUNCH LADY. But we can't find out about her without permission to look!"

I see Emily's dilemma—no, *our* dilemma!

What are we going to do?

Chapter Nine

Past Meets Present

EMILY'S RIGHT. WITHOUT PERMISSION WE'RE STUCK.
If only we could get Principal Gilamon to agree
to let us look at those files.

Then it hits me. "I have an idea."

I lean over Principal Gilamon's desk. The
closer I get to him the worse he smells—like
rotten lunch meat! Yuck! Holding my nose, I lean
in close to his ear.

"Principal Gilamon," I say. "May my sister
Emily and I please have permission to read the
files for Fillmore Middle School? If the answer
is yes, just grunt."

I wait for a second. Nothing happens.

Then zombie Gilamon looks me right in the eye and grunts.

Emily squeals with delight.

"Brilliant, Billy! This is perfect! And I recorded it so we have the proof!"

I turn to Mom. "Is that okay?" I ask. "Does that count as official permission?"

Mom hesitates, but nods. "Excellent spy skills, Billy!" she says. "Come on!" (Though I should mention, unless the principal at your school has turned into a zombie, do *not* by any means go through your school's files.)

We all go into the records room. Old metal file cabinets line every wall. There must be twenty of them! The room is dark. It has no windows, and the overhead fluorescents make everything look yellow.

Mom opens her briefcase and pulls out what looks like a large coin, maybe the size of a half-dollar. She flips the coin over and it expands into a flashlight, shining a bright beam.

"One of Xavier's inventions?" I ask.

Mom nods.

She sweeps the light around the room. It reveals file drawers labeled TEACHERS, EXAMS, CLIPPINGS, and on and on. Many of the drawers have no labels at all.

The four of us dig in, opening drawers and grabbing files at random. Mom, Emily, and I start flipping through them, one by one. Agent Paul does the same thing, and I immediately see why he is an important part of this spy mission.

While the three of us each use our two hands, Agent Paul uses all eight of his arms and suction cups to flip through eight files at once, being careful not to get any of the papers wet.

"I think I found something!" Mom exclaims a few minutes later, aiming her flashlight at a far corner of the room.

The small pool of light reveals a drawer labeled: CAFETERIA PERSONNEL.

Mom pulls open the drawer. It squeaks and whines as it slides along its rusty track. The

drawer is packed with files on decades of former Fillmore Middle School employees. As Mom grabs a handful of files, dust falls off the sides.

No one has looked at these for a *long* time!

"Okay, we've narrowed our search," Mom says. "Everyone grab a handful—or a tentacleful—and start looking."

We all take a few files and start flipping through the papers. It's like HAUNTED

LUNCH MENUS OF THE PAST in here—we find recipes for tuna supreme, hot dog casserole, pork and bean surprise. And I thought *Dad* makes weird food!

After another few minutes Agent Paul speaks through the Paul-O-Phone.

"Take a look at this," he says.

Floating to the top of his tank, Agent Paul reaches a tentacle out and hands me a file. I look it over and see that it is labeled COOKS, CASHIERS, DIRECTORS OF CAFETERIA SERVICES. There's a stamp on it—from this year!

I pull out the file on the current director of Cafeteria Services.

"Her name is Johanna Brown," I say. Same last name as Petula—well, I suppose I could have guessed that. "Hmm . . . she was a student here at Fillmore about twenty years ago. But I don't see anything strange about her on this info sheet."

Emily flips my sheet over. Nope. Nothing.

"Well, if she was a student at Fillmore Middle, she must have a permanent record,"

Emily says. "Here—let's search the student archive. Maybe we can find something there."

Emily and Mom dart to the other side of the room. They're quick. Soon enough, they pull out a big messy file on Johanna Brown. I guess my teachers weren't kidding—you really *do* have a permanent record!

Emily takes out a newspaper clipping.

"Bingo!" she cries. "Look at this. It's a clipping from the print edition of *Right Next Door* from twenty years ago."

Everyone huddles round Emily. Agent Paul peers through the glass of his tank.

ALL-STAR ATHLETE EXPELLED
FROM SCHOOL

by Kathleen Silvestri

Fillmore Middle School's beloved all-star track athlete, Johanna Brown, was expelled today. As it turns out, this track diva is more than just a superstar athlete—she's a bit of a scientist in disguise, too!

Brown was conducting an unauthorized experiment in her chemistry class at Fillmore Middle School when her formula went wrong. She set out to create a new sports drink for runners to use after a race, but when she tested it on the track team, it burned off the hair of many kids in class—plus the principal's hair—and almost set the whole school on fire!

What will be next for this former all-star? Who knows? Only time will tell, though if you ask this reporter, I don't think that's the last we'll hear of Johanna Brown.

"Oh, wow," says Emily. "Kathleen Silvestri must be Kathy Jenkins before she got married.

On my class schedule it shows that her middle initial is *S*."

"Kathy has been writing for *Right Next Door* for a very long time," says Mom. I think she's a little impressed—Mom changes missions so often, the idea must sound really foreign to her.

"Getting expelled sounds awful," I say, suddenly feeling sorry for Johanna. "I mean, she was just an inventor trying to make something to help people. Kind of like what I do. I get it that her invention went really, really wrong, but I've been there before too. Expelling someone is pretty harsh. I wonder if there's anything we can do to help her?"

"That's sweet, honey," Mom says. "I'm all for helping Johanna, but right now, she may be taking out her revenge by hurting *a lot* of innocent people. Now that we know the history, Suspect A has become even more of a suspect. We need to go right to the source of our current problem and figure things out."

"*TO THE KITCHEN!*" Agent Paul screeches.

Mom, Emily, and I all nod. "Let's go," we say together.

We move quietly past Principal Gilamon, who continues to stamp papers and groan softly. As we leave, I see Mr. Hairston is still scribbling on some forms. He doesn't look up.

As the four of us hurry through the halls, we squeeze past zombie students. No one is surprised at all to see a high schooler, a parent, and an octopus here.

In the cafeteria the main lunchroom is empty. Huh, I guess that makes sense—it's still an hour away from lunch period, after all. Hurrying through the big room, we push open the swinging doors and head right into the cafeteria's kitchen.

Once there, I stop in my tracks. Everyone on the lunch staff is now GREEN!

The cafeteria staff is all zombified. They work together slowly, moving stiffly, groaning and grunting as they put together the day's lunch.

And just like in Principal Gilamon's office,

no one seems to notice that two teenagers, a parent, and an octopus have just waltzed right into their kitchen. Looking over the staff, I spot a woman who doesn't look like the others.

Her skin is green, but it's not the same green as everyone else. It looks like she put green makeup on her skin, to disguise herself, maybe. She is busy slicing the nasty lunch meat, but I notice that she is wearing protective gloves.

This must be Johanna!

"I think we found her," I whisper to Mom, pointing. I take a deep breath. I guess it's time to get down to business. I decide to walk right up to her.

"Johanna? Johanna Brown?" I ask, as kindly as possible. Despite all the trouble she's caused, I *do* feel sorry for her. "My name is Billy Sure. I'm an inventor too, and I'd like to talk to you."

The woman looks confused. She also looks nervous. It's obvious that she is *not* a zombie, though—aside from her green makeup, she clearly heard and understood what I just said.

She looks around anxiously, like she doesn't want to get caught doing something wrong.

"I'm not Johanna," she whispers quietly, looking back over her shoulder, then past me. "But if you're looking for Johanna, I suggest you don't. I suggest you leave RIGHT NOW. You don't want to mess with Johanna. She's very scary. I'm just pretending to be one of her zombie minions so she doesn't know that I haven't really turned."

"Is there something scary about her *besides* turning everyone into zombies?" Emily asks.

The woman looks left, then right, her lips trembling.

"There are rumors about Johanna," she says softly. "Terrible rumors. You should get out while you still can."

"We know about Johanna," I explain. "That's why we want to find her. I think we can—"

The woman's eyes open wide in terror, just as I feel a blast of COLD BREATH on my neck!

Emily shrieks. Mom takes a step back,

assuming a combat-ready pose. Agent Paul spins around in his tank, thrashing, churning up the water.

I turn around and find myself face to face with a woman wearing a name tag that reads DIRECTOR OF CAFETERIA SERVICES.

It's Johanna! She's found us. Are we doomed?!

Chapter Ten

The Truth at Last

THE NERVOUS GREEN-SKINNED WOMAN WE'D BEEN speaking with looks at me with sad, frightened eyes. Then she turns and hurries from the kitchen.

Johanna, a tall woman with dark graying hair and wrinkled (not green) skin looks us over.

"HMPH," she grumbles. "I thought *everyone* at Fillmore would be a zombie by now. But I guess I was wrong."

"So you admit that you're the one trying to turn everyone into zombies!" I shout.

I honestly can't believe that she just came right out and said it. I don't feel sorry for Johanna at all anymore!

I turn to Emily, who has her phone in her hand.

"Em, are you getting all this?" I ask.

Emily nods. We've got a recorded confession and everything! This is turning out to be easier that I thought!

Johanna frowns.

"I'm only trying to prove to Fillmore Middle School what no one else allowed me to prove—that I'm the best inventor this school has ever seen, *and* the fastest runner!" Johanna screeches, scowling at all of us.

But she's not finished yet.

"When I went to school here, I tried to invent a new sports drink to help athletes recover their energy after a tough race or a big game," she says. "But it . . . it had some issues."

"Yeah, we read all about it," I say. "You were expelled. We know."

"I was just trying to help, and to win for the

school," Johanna continues. "Did I deserve to be punished for that?"

"Maybe not," I say. "But what you're doing now is not right. These kids—my friends, my teachers, my business partner, and your niece!—they didn't do anything to you. They don't deserve this."

Johanna is unconvinced.

"The school should have encouraged me, believed in me," Johanna continues. "But they didn't. They kicked me out right before the track championships. I had a chance. I could have won. But now it's time for my revenge—now I've got to make sure that everyone here moves slowly. I'll be the fastest, once again!" She laughs.

I can see that there is no way Johanna is going to listen to reason.

It's funny: The crazier Johanna seems, the more I feel like I understand her. Maybe because she's a fellow inventor? I mean, I had a terrible time trying to make some of my inventions work the way I wanted. The

Cat-Dog Translator was a disaster and almost got *me* kicked out of Fillmore. Nobody gets it right all the time—but that's also one of the fun parts of inventing.

Wait a minute. I have an idea.

"Johanna, listen to me," I say. "I'm an inventor too, and I've also messed up inventions. I've caused some big trouble with my inventions right here at Fillmore. Even for Principal Gilamon."

Johanna looks right at me. Maybe she's really listening.

"What if you came to work with me at Sure Things, Inc. as an inventor?" I say. "We can still achieve your dream—only different! You'll be fast, fair and square."

Mom and Emily look at me like *I'm* the one who's a little crazy. Even Agent Paul swishes a bit in his tank and opens his big octopus eyes really wide.

"Of course, you'd have to UNZOMBIE everyone here first," I continue. "But if you do, the school will be back to normal, and you'll be able to use your inventing talent for good. What do you think?"

Mom smiles at me. I think at first she was surprised and a bit confused by my offer, but now I think she's proud of me for trying to find a good way out of this.

Only, Johanna won't have any of it.

"I don't need your pity!" Johanna cries. "I don't need to work with you—a lousy *kid* inventor! I just need my REVENGE!"

Mom steps forward.

"In that case, there's nothing left to do," she says in a very direct voice. Wow. Mom is a total champ. "Johanna Brown, you are under arrest."

Mom squeezes the ring from her briefcase and it expands into handcuffs. But before she can put the cuffs on Johanna, the crazed cafeteria lady snatches a piece of the mystery meat off a tray . . . and tosses it into Agent Paul's tank!

"NO!" Mom shouts.

The water in Agent Paul's tank starts churning, swirling, and turning green.

"The lunch meat is going to poison the water—this stuff is going to hit Agent Paul *really* quick," Mom explains to Emily and me.

"Exactly! Now this octopus will become a zombie!" Johanna cackles wildly. Then she turns and looks at all of us. "In fact, now that you *all* know about what I have done, you *all* have to become zombies too!"

Her eyes turn on me.

"Billy Sure, you are next!" Johanna screeches, tossing a piece of mystery meat right at my face!

But before the meat can hit my mouth, Emily jumps in front of me. The lunch meat hits Emily in the face and slides down her cheek, leaving a SLIMY GREEN trail behind. Then it drops to the floor.

"I have to make sure that you don't become a zombie, Billy!" Emily shouts. "You're the only one who can invent an antidote to the mystery meat. If you become the last nonzombie kid at Fillmore Middle School, it'll all be up to you!"

Before I have a chance to thank Emily for

putting *just* a little bit of pressure on me to save everyone, the water in Agent Paul's tank stops moving! It is now bright green—and so is Agent Paul—oh no, Agent Paul . . .

. . . is now a full-fledged OCTOPUS ZOMBIE! Most likely (though I haven't done any research on it), the only one in the entire world.

Then with a powerful push, Agent Paul's big green head pops out of the water. Since he's a zombie, he no longer needs to be in the tank. He can attack at will!

"Behold, the ZOMBOCTOPUS!" Johanna cries.

If this were a movie, the person in charge of sound effects would have programmed lightning to hit at that exact moment. But this is *not* a movie—and that's what makes this all the more terrifying.

I can't tell if Johanna is proud of her Zomboctopus creation or a little surprised that her mystery meat worked on Agent Paul. I'm going to guess both.

Agent Paul drops to the ground with a loud green **SPLAT!** He stands in front of me, Mom, and Emily. Wow—I never noticed before. Agent Paul is taller than Mom! Wait a minute . . . is zombie Paul getting 𝔹𝕀𝔾𝔾𝔼ℝ?

Mom steps right up to him.

"Paul!" she yells. "We're partners! You can't do this! We're on a serious mission! You need to get back into your tank."

But Agent Paul keeps coming, slithering right at us. We back up slowly. I turn around, looking for a way out. It's no use. Our backs are now against the wall. We're trapped!

One of Agent Paul's tentacles reaches out to grab me.

This is the end! I think, *swallowed whole by a Zomboctopus!*

Blam!

From out of nowhere, a loaf of bread comes sailing through the air! And it's not just any old loaf of bread; it's an institutional-sized 𝕄𝔼𝔾𝔸𝕃𝕆𝔸𝔽 with about two hundred slices in it! The bread smashes right into Agent

Paul, taking him by surprise and making him lose his balance. He tumbles right to the floor.

"Go! Run!" shouts a voice from across the kitchen. "Get out—now!"

I look across the room and see the first woman we spoke with—the one with the green makeup, who was only pretending to be a zombie and who warned us about Johanna.

We don't need to be told twice. Mom, Emily, and I dash from the kitchen and cut back through the cafeteria. We push past crowds of zombie students and race as fast as we can out of the building.

When we are several blocks away, we finally stop running.

"THAT WAS HORRIBLE!" I cry, trying to catch my breath. "Poor Agent Paul. I hope he'll be okay. Em, did you get all that recorded? We need to go speak with Kathy about getting this story published as quickly as possible, so everyone knows what's going on at Fillmore. She knows everything going on locally—she must think something is up. We have to warn people. Meanwhile, I'll get working on an antidote. Sound good? Em?"

Emily says nothing.

"EM?" I ask again, glancing over at her.

Mom looks up too.

That's when we see it. *No!*

Emily's face is all green! When she jumped in front of me, some of the mystery meat must have gotten into her mouth when it hit her face!

Mom sees what's going on and instantly springs into action. She grabs Emily's phone, which is still recording, and hands it to me.

"I think it's time we all go to HQ and work on putting an end to this," she says, a little too calmly.

Huh. I guess when you've spent your career saving the world from terrible disasters, a few zombies—even when one happens to be an octopus and another is your daughter—don't faze you.

Mom and I hurry to the office. When we've gotten a few blocks from the school I look around but don't see Emily.

"I think we lost Emily, Mom," I say.

She stops and looks back, and we see Emily several blocks away, walking toward us in that strange slow, stiff-legged zombie walk.

"What do we do, Mom?" I ask. I don't want to leave Emily on her own—who knows where she might wander off to—but I need to start working on an antidote as soon as I can.

Before Mom can reply, Emily shouts, "Luuuunch meeeeeat!"

Mom shakes her head.

"There's nothing we can do for her here, Billy," she says. She sounds calm, but I realize now that she's pretty nervous—I never knew I got my anxious twitchy leg thing from her. "The only thing to do is get to HQ as fast as possible and get working on a cure."

A few minutes later Mom and I arrive at HQ. We walk through the front door and see Manny sitting at his desk. He stares blankly at us. Ewww. Is that a POOL OF DROOL on his chin?!

"Hello, Manny," says Mom.

"Gurruggh," Manny groans.

"Well, that's not very polite," Mom laughs.

At least she's managed to have a sense of humor in this!

Gurruggh

"You'd better get to work," Mom tells me. "You can do it, honey."

I text Jada and Nat to give them an update, but I don't hear back. Great. Just when I need to talk to them, Kevin is probably hogging all of Jada's attention. Then I settle in at my workbench. I know Mom's words are encouraging, but honestly, this might be the MOST NERVOUS I've ever been for an invention. Even more than when we had to save Agent Paul during my time at Spy Academy. The fate of almost *everyone* I know is at stake!

I work for an hour or so, mixing in lots of different random ingredients. Most of them are really yummy things like chocolate-sprinkle cupcakes. Because if you asked me what's the opposite of ooey-gooey mysterious lunch meat, it's definitely chocolate-sprinkle cupcakes.

But is it going to work?!

Chapter Eleven

Zombie Zap

THERE'S ONLY ONE WAY TO FIND OUT IF THIS ANTIDOTE
works. I have to test it.

I put the antidote into a
spray bottle, like we used for
the INVISIBILITY SPRAY.
Then I hold it up next to a
sample of the mysterious lunch
meat (after stepping outside HQ
to keep my zombie partner from
smelling it) and spritz it on.

chhhh!

Strangely, the spray doesn't look like a

liquid, which is what I expected. It looks more like green crazy string! It wraps and coils itself around the nasty lunch meat.

A few seconds later the string turns white and then vanishes. The lunch meat looks normal again. Okay, it may be a little old and a little dry . . . but not a hint of green anywhere!

This is a good sign. But now that I've tested it on the lunch meat, I've got to test it on an ACTUAL ZOMBIE.

"Good luck," I whisper to myself.

I slip back into the office carrying the anti-dote in one hand and the piece of unzombied meat in the other. Manny doesn't seem to notice that I—or, more importantly, the meat—have returned.

"How'd you do?" Mom asks. She stares intently at her smartphone. I wonder if her other spy colleagues know about this outbreak.

I hold up the piece of soppy lunch meat and explain that although I'm not sure, I *think* it worked.

"That's great, Billy!" Mom says. "Why don't you try it on Emily first? She's been a zombie for less time than Manny. It might be easier to change her back."

Well, a parent's permission to use the antidote on her daughter is as good as any. Mom dashes off to find Emily and brings her to HQ quick. I walk over to my workbench, where Mom sat her down, and realize Emily looks kind of like a broken paper doll. There's drool on her chin too. If I weren't so afraid for her, I'd take a picture and post this on InstaInstaChat. She may be a zombie, but she's still my annoying older sister!

"Okay, here goes," I say.

Mom gives me a thumbs up.

I spray some of my invention onto Emily's arm, and the green crazy string wraps itself gently around her wrist. A few seconds later, the string turns white, then vanishes, showing that Emily's arm now looks normal too!

"So far, so good!" I say. Then I spray my invention—I'm going to call it ZOMBIE

ZAP—all over Emily, until she is covered from head to toe in green string!

The string turns white and disappears. Just as I'm wondering if this is going to work, Emily blinks open her eyes! She looks directly at Mom and at me.

"I'M FREE!!" Emily shrieks. "Billy, you did it! You invented the antidote! Now we can save the whole school. We can cure them of the effects of the zombie lunch meat . . ." Emily pauses, like she's suddenly remembered something very important. Then her body slumps. The drool returns.

"Luuuunch meeeeeat!"

Emily's skin bubbles and turns back to a sickly green. It seems like as quickly as she was healed, she's turned back into a zombie again.

"Well, I usually don't get my inventions right on the first try," I say. "On to prototype number two. Now I have to find a way to make the Zombie Zap permanent."

Mom nods. She goes back to typing on her smartphone.

I return to my workbench and start tweaking

the Zombie Zap. I've honestly never felt pressure quite like this before. I've got to save everyone—my friends, my business partner, my mom's partner, my teachers and principal, and, of course, my older sister!

I barely notice as someone enters the back door of the office.

"Billy, look who's here," Mom says.

Mom must have invited someone super smart. But who?

I turn around.

Standing in my office is KATHY JENKINS!

Kathy Jenkins?! The *Right Next Door* reporter? Emily's Journalism teacher, Kathy Jenkins?

I'm stunned! And a little nervous. What's Kathy doing over here? The *last* thing I need right now is another mean article about Sure Things, Inc.

Kathy waltzes in like she is queen of Sure Things, Inc. HQ. She doesn't even bother to say hello. Or knock. But what's weird . . . she looks visibly upset. I've never seen Kathy upset before. Usually, she loves drama—drama makes for better stories. So, what could possibly be going on to make *Kathy Jenkins* upset?!

"Billy, it's my daughter," Kathy says, matter-of-fact. "Samantha is . . . well, she's just not herself lately. It's like there's something *majorly* wrong with her. I tried interviewing her to find out, but . . ."

Hmm. Now I feel kind of bad for Samantha. I can't imagine growing up and feeling like you're on an interview all the time.

Interview? That's when I notice that Kathy doesn't have her trusty notepad with her. Like Emily's new thing, Kathy carries that notepad *everywhere*. It's where she records her stories. She must really be upset. Usually Kathy scribbles away on it constantly!

"I posted in the Parent-Teacher group on the school website, and some of the others kids' parents are concerned too," Kathy says, showing me a website on her smartphone. "I did some research and it seems that there may be something wrong with the new director of Cafeteria Services at Fillmore. Then your mom found me on the group and invited me out here. Do you know anything about this?" she finishes.

"Well, there's definitely something wrong with the director," I say, pulling out Emily's phone. "And here's the proof."

I play back the recording we made at the school, which tells the entire story, most of it right from Johanna's own lips. Kathy's eyes open wide. We aren't even close to the end of the recording when it all clicks for her.

"JOHANNA . . . BROWN," she says, like she's remembering something from twenty years ago. Oh yeah—because she probably is! "Johanna Brown wants revenge—and she wants it on all of Fillmore Middle School! I always thought she was a little strange, even back when I knew her as a student. But I never thought she would do something like this. We have to stop her!"

"I may be close to being able to do that," I say. "I just invented an antidote called Zombie Zap. If I can get it to work permanently, we can cure everyone and take down Johanna."

"Thank you, Billy," says Kathy. She looks . . . almost like she's about to cry? "I know Samantha would be thanking you too, if she weren't—"

"Urghhh," Manny drawls.

"What he said." She shrugs her shoulders.

Mom stands up and gives Kathy a hug.

"We're going to get through this," she says. "In the meantime, Kathy, we have to focus on putting all of our unique talents to the test. Why don't you start on an article, exposing Johanna for what she's done? You can use Emily's audio clip."

Kathy nods.

"That's an excellent idea," she says, pocketing Emily's phone. "I'll get to work."

Mom leads Kathy out of HQ. When Mom comes back, she's still scrolling through the parent group comments on the website.

"A lot of parents are concerned. I'm worried about Mr. and Dr. Reyes. I need to talk to them about what's going on," says Mom. "You keep working, Billy—we'll put a stop to this before it's a NATIONAL EPIDEMIC."

Mom heads into the Reyes' house. I turn back to my workbench and pull a few more things out of the drawers and bins.

"A few drops of purple ink, some ground-up seaweed, and four green gummy bears," I say, adding each thing to the formula. As I wait for the new ingredients to blend with the original formula, Mom returns.

"I spoke with Dr. Reyes," Mom says, looking over at Manny. He continues to mindlessly stare at his computer screen. "She thanked me for filling her in on what's going on. She told me that Manny has spent days in the office before, but this time they knew something was really wrong."

"Urrrgh!" comes a cry from the far corner of the office.

I look over and see Emily stumbling around the office, back in her zombie trance. "Hurrrr," she moans.

Manny looks around and adds "Urgshh,

gruurr!" It's almost like they're having a weird zombie conversation.

I don't know about you, but I'm kinda glad Philo isn't here right now. I can't help but think he'd be barking along!

"Billy, I think I need to take Emily home," Mom says.

"Actually, I think working in my bedroom for now might be best," I say, gathering up everything I need. "That way I don't have to listen to Manny groan."

Back at home a short while later, I feel my eyes start to close. I can't believe how late it is. Dad brings me a snack, POACHED EGGS WITH PEANUT BUTTER, which actually isn't half bad—or maybe I'm so tired I don't even notice the taste.

This whole zombie thing has been exhausting, to say the least. I haven't slept well in days. My head drifts down to the surface of the workbench . . . slowly . . . and I fall into a dream.

"Ruff! Ruff! Ruff!"

I blink open my eyes. Philo has leaped onto my bed and is now licking my face.

"Boy, what are you doing—" I start to say, trying to push him off, when I look outside. The sun is out! I must have slept the whole night, and I didn't even work on the Zombie Zap.

Oh no. What kind of inventor am I?!

Wait a minute.

That is *exactly* what kind of inventor I am! I sleep-invent! It's one of the things that makes Billy Sure so "sure" about inventing. I leap out of bed excitedly and check my desk for blueprints.

SURE ENOUGH, there are completed blueprints for the Zombie Zap on my desk!!

I sit down and look over the blueprints. They make perfect sense. I can't believe I didn't see what I needed to fix the antidote before.

I roll up the blueprints and rush downstairs, to where Mom and Emily are. Mom explains that Dad is meeting with a famous art curator this morning, so she didn't want to bother him. It looks like neither Mom nor Emily got any sleep last night. Mom's eyes make her look almost like a zombie too!

Zombie Emily is making a mess. She's going through the fridge, the pantry, and all the cabinets, pulling out anything that is green. A jar of pickles, a green cup, an avocado, some old food that Dad made last week, and a package of split peas are piled onto the kitchen table.

Mom tries to keep up with her, grabbing the stuff from the table and putting it away. But every time Mom takes something from the table, Emily puts down something else.

"Mom, I got it!" I shout.

"Got what?" she asks.

Shoving aside a lime, a green plate, and a bowl of mint chocolate chip ice cream, I unroll my blueprint on the kitchen table.

"The permanent antidote!" I say. "I sleep-invented it last night."

"Oh, honey," Mom says. She really *does* sound exhausted. "That is great news. We've got to get you to the Sure Things, Inc. Headquarters so you can make some right away. And we'll need to take Emily to cure her. Emily?"

Zombie Emily looks up.

"Do you want to see some *green lights* on the drive over to Manny's?"

Glop.

A big splatter of drool drops down from Emily's mouth. I think that's excitement—for zombie Emily, anyway.

Mom takes Emily by the hand and leads her to the front door.

"Come on, boy!" I shout to Philo. "Let's go help Manny!"

Emily, Philo, and I pile into Mom's car. We speed off toward the office. Emily sits in the front passenger seat, next to Mom. She opens the glove compartment and starts rummaging around. She pulls out a green emergency flashlight and a pair of green driving gloves. She also points excitedly at every green light.

Mom just shakes her head and speeds up.

A few minutes later we arrive at Manny's.

"I have to tell Manny that I sleep-invented the cure," I say as we get out of the car. "Or at least tell Mr. and Dr. Reyes. We'll need their permission to use it on Manny since it's still technically in the prototype stages."

We head over to the house, Philo at my side, Mom leading zombie Emily. Inside we find Manny and his parents.

"We couldn't let him go to school like this," says Mr. Reyes. "He's been doing this all morning."

Manny stumbles around the house, opening drawers, cabinets, the refrigerator, anything he can open, the whole time moaning "'LUUUNCH MEEEAT!'" Like Emily, he seems to have piled an assortment of green things on the counter.

I see more creamed spinach than I'd know what to do with.

"Well, I have good news," I tell them. "I have the blueprints for a permanent cure right here."

"Then I'd say you better get busy!" says a voice from the front door. Hey, wait a second. I know that voice! I could recognize it anywhere!

"Jada!" I cry. "What are you doing here?"

Chapter Twelve

a Surely-Definite Victory!

JADA AND HER BUSINESS PARTNER, NAT DEFINITE, stand in the doorway.

Nat turns to me. "You really need to learn to use your *inside voice*, Billy," she says. "We could hear you from a mile away."

Hey, it's not my fault I get loud when I'm excited. Still, I'm so glad to see them. Jada pulls me into a hug, and that same chill goes up my spine.

Everyone walks into the garage and takes a seat. Manny's parents help him out to his desk, and Mom trails after Emily. After a few minutes, I've completed the revisions to the Zombie Zap formula. I load this new prototype into a spray bottle.

"Okay, this is it," I say nervously. "Who should I spray first?"

"Urghhh," Manny grunts.

"Looks like we have a volunteer," Nat smiles.

Mr. and Dr. Reyes look nervously at each other, then nod to me. "If anyone can do this, you can," they say. Their words are very encouraging.

I try not to think about how much is really at stake here. This is THE MOST IMPORTANT INVENTION I'VE MADE YET!

Zurp!

I spray some of what I hope will be the permanent version of Zombie Zap on Manny. The green string covers his body. This time, the string glows!

"Come on, partner, I miss the real you!" I say.

Everyone stares at Manny. Nothing happens. I start to pace back and forth. What if this formula is also a dud? What will I do then?

After a few minutes I notice the glowing stop. The crazy string vanishes, and Manny looks a little less green.

"Manny?" I whisper.

"Gurrugg," he groans.

I feel my heart sink. The Zombie Zap didn't work.

Manny continues to moan. "Luuunch meeat," he says.

Mr. and Dr. Reyes sigh. This must be really upsetting to them.

Manny looks at me.

"Billy—lunch meat," he says, this time very clearly.

Billy? He said my name? He said my name! Now that sounds like the REAL Manny!

"Hey, does anybody have a turkey sandwich? Really, any sandwich will do. I'm starving!" Manny smiles.

"Manny!" I cry. "You're back!" I turn around and see that the green in Manny's skin is completely gone.

Everyone in the room claps. Mr. and Dr. Reyes get up and scoop Manny up into a big hug.

"Where have I been?" Manny asks. "I feel like I've been away. But I don't really understand. And why am I craving a turkey sandwich?"

I quickly remind Manny of all that's happened.

"I remember it now," Manny says. "This is why we tested the lunch meat on me and not you. I knew you could do it, partner!"

In the midst of all of this, Mom grabs the bottle of Zombie Zap and sprays Emily down. Emily looks dazed for a few minutes. Then her eyes open wide and her skin returns to its normal color!

"Emily?" Mom says.

Emily doesn't say anything at first. She doesn't look confused. She looks . . . almost mad.

Before saying anything, Emily reaches behind her ear and feels that nothing is there. "WHAT HAPPENED TO MY PENCIL?!" Emily screeches.

Yep. That's my sister, all right. I laugh, and that's when it hits her.

"Billy, you did it! You found the antidote!"

"We have to go cure everyone else now—the whole school and Agent Paul," says Mom. "Billy, how fast can you make a big batch of this?"

And that's when my happy mood is suddenly shattered.

"I'm not sure, Mom," I say. "It took *a long time* to get the formula just right and make a small sample. Mass producing it? That's a whole other thing. Usually Manny plans that for weeks, but I bet he hasn't been doing much work lately."

Manny smiles nervously.

"Good bet," he says, through gritted teeth. I wonder if it feels weird to have control of your body again.

"Well, that's where we come in," Jada says, smiling. She turns to Nat, who nods. "If you give Nat the formula, Billy, Definite Devices can handle the mass production—I promise."

"And I promise that there'll be no funny business," Nat adds. "Those days are long gone."

"I'm afraid we're not much help anymore," Dr. Reyes says, looking at her husband and all of us. "Unless, of course, you need something with feet! We'll be back inside. Manny, we are so proud of you for volunteering to save the school, but please don't do that again without consulting us first." She smiles at her son. "Good luck, Team Sure Things, Inc.! May the ZAP be with you."

Manny's parents walk back into their house.

I hand my blueprints and Zombie Zap sample over to Jada and Nat. They hurry off to the Definite Devices office to begin production. While they're gone, I bring Manny and Emily up to speed on everything that has happened. It also helps explain why Emily doesn't have her phone, because Kathy's got it.

"I can't believe that Kathy Jenkins is basing her story on my recording," Emily says, as if that's the most important thing here.

About an hour later, Nat and Jada return.

"We're all set," Jada says calmly. "Mission SAVE FILLMORE MIDDLE SCHOOL—let's go!"

Mom, Emily, Manny, Nat, Jada, and I head to the school. "See ya later, boy," I tell Philo. He barely stirs from his doggy bed—it's been an exhausting few days for him, too.

As Mom drives us to school, I realize that I don't see anything that looks like large amounts of Zombie Zap, or a way to get it to everyone that needs it. Jada is empty-handed, and Nat is wearing a normal-looking backpack.

Jada sees my worried look. It feels kind of nice to know she can pick up what I'm feeling.

"Don't worry," she says. "Wait until you see what Nat invented!"

We arrive at Fillmore Middle School. I'm stunned by what I see. It's really like something out of a science-fiction movie!

Agent Paul has grown to *gigantic* size. He's sitting on top of the school with his huge tentacles wrapped around the whole building! This must be some weird side effect of the lunch meat that only affects sea creatures. Or octopuses. As far as I know, Agent Paul's the only nonhuman that has been infected.

"Agent Paul!" Mom shouts.

I can tell she is horrified by what she sees. This is her partner. Like Manny is mine.

Although it's not funny, the thought of Manny with a bunch of tentacles, blown up to the size of a small spacecraft and sitting menacingly atop Fillmore Middle School makes me laugh.

Mom turns to me. "Agent Paul's so big, we're going to need a *lot* of Zombie Zap for him—and for the rest of the school!"

She's right. But even if we somehow magically have enough Zombie Zap, I have no idea
how we can get it all the way up to Agent Paul!

"I've got it!" Jada shouts. She opens Nat's
backpack and pulls out a small metal contraption that looks like a canister vacuum cleaner.
It has a long hose attached to it.

"Nat just invented a bunch of these—they're
called ZOMBIE ZAPPERS. They're ready and
loaded with tons and tons of your Zombie Zap.
And the small canisters are pressurized so the
streams will reach a long way."

I look at Nat. She smiles.

"When you need a zap, who are you going to
call?" she laughs. "Definite Devices."

After all the trouble Nat has caused Manny,
Sure Things, Inc., and me in the past, I guess
this time she really *is* on our side.

"Since your Zombie Zap helped Manny, it's
time to help everyone else, too," Nat says. She
has a Zombie Zapper strapped across her back,
reaches into her bag, and hands others to us.

"Aim the hose directly at Agent Paul," Nat

instructs. "He'll be the first zombie we take down, since he's the biggest. Okay? Ready . . . set . . . go!"

ZURP!

I squeeze a button on the hose. Instantly, a stream of green crazy string comes shooting out! It races through the air, reaching all the way to the top of the school. When it gets to Agent Paul, it wraps itself around him and all eight of his zombie tentacles.

Will it work? I don't know. It worked on Emily and Manny. Here's to hoping it works on a giant octopus, too!

Agent Paul is still HUGE, but he looks a little less green. Which I guess isn't saying much, since, as an octopus, Agent Paul is always changing color.

Suddenly, Agent Paul's eyes widen. His eyes dart to his tentacles, each one still thrashing against the school!

"What−?" Agent Paul bellows. "WHAT IN ATLANTIS AM I DOING?!"

"Quick, Nat!" Jada yells. Nat doesn't need

to be told twice. Agent Paul's mind might be back, but his body is still ZOMBIFIED! Nat switches her Zombie Zapper to FULL BLAST.

Nat tosses lots more Zombie Zap up to Agent Paul.

It's amazing how much Zombie Zap fits into her backpack. I'll have to remember to ask her if she's invented a special backpack with unlimited room inside. That would be a pretty cool invention!

Nat's extra Zombie Zap seems to do the trick!

Agent Paul starts shrinking.

"Paul!" Mom shouts. It almost looks like there are tears in her eyes. I bet she feels a little less alone—Agent Paul and Mom are the only *real* spies here, as far as I know.

Agent Paul climbs down the building and scoots next to Mom. Maybe not *all* of the zombieism has worn off, though, because he doesn't need his tank. Well, we'll work on that later.

"Onward!" Jada shouts.

With Nat leading the way, we all charge into the school. It feels kind of like we're in an action movie.

Everywhere we turn, we spray students and teachers with Zombie Zap. Agent Paul grabs eight canisters at once with his tentacles and creates an unstoppable antizombie fountain.

The hall fills with green glowing string crisscrossing in every direction. In a few minutes, almost everyone at Fillmore Middle School is back to normal. Jada finishes up the rest.

"WE DID IT!" I shout.

Everyone cheers. Though some of the recently zombified students are a little slow to move, they do their best to dance and cheer along.

But our celebration is short lived.

"You did *WHAT*?" comes a shrill voice.

I spin around and see Johanna Brown. She comes RIGHT TOWARD ME!

"What is this? You can't take away my legion of zombies! Put that spray away. You can't do this in my school! I am the *director of Cafeteria Services!*" She waves a spatula in the air at us.

At that exact moment, Jada finishes spraying Principal Gilamon. Principal Gilamon's Mohawk turns back from being green to being bright purple. He blinks rapidly, looks at me, then salutes. He strides up to Johanna.

"You mean, you *were* the director of Cafeteria Services," Principal Gilamon says. "Johanna Brown, on behalf of the school board, it is my duty to expel you from the Fillmore Middle School grounds—again!

"We tried to give you a second chance—we really did. And I might even be able to look past this zombie nonsense . . ." Principal Gilamon pauses. "But now that I think about it, this all started when my hair turned purple, and I think you did *that* as well!"

Principal Gilamon points to his purple Mohawk.

"I remember eating a purple muffin from the school cafeteria on your first day here," he continues. "I thought it was whimsical, but now I see that you were just testing your revenge scheme on me!"

Johanna looks shocked, like she can't believe she's been found out. Remember when I felt kinda bad for her? Yeah, I don't feel bad anymore . . . AT ALL!

"And so," Principal Gilamon says, "it is my GREAT PLEASURE to appoint the *new* director of Cafeteria Services at Fillmore Middle School—Zohra Azeem!"

Principal Gilamon turns. He smiles at the only woman in the entire building who looks green. It's the same woman from the cafeteria, the one who saved us! She's still wearing her green makeup.

"Thank you so much, Principal Gilamon," Zohra says, smiling. "I'll do my best to make you—and this school—proud."

Petula makes her way over to us. Now that she's no longer a zombie and back to being regular swim captain and Drama Club President Petula, she moves pretty fast.

"Nice to see you back to normal," I say.

Petula smiles at me but doesn't say anything else. She walks right up to her dear ol' Aunt Johanna.

"I can't believe you would do this," she says to her. "I TRUSTED you! I told my friends to trust you! I was *so* happy you got this job.

Now I'm going to have to tell Grandma all about it."

I can see Johanna's expression change. She looks really upset.

I guess no matter how old you are, you're always gonna be afraid of getting told on to your parents!

The crowd makes its way over. Some kids stick their tongues out at Johanna. Some kids thank me, Nat, Jada, Emily, Mom, Manny, and Agent Paul. A few of them remark on Agent Paul's . . . well, octopus-ness.

"Is that a side effect of the Zombie Zap?" Peter asks. "Are we all going to turn into octopuses?!"

Man, I would love to prank Peter.

"Whoops," I say, shrugging. "Guess we'll all be octopuses soon!"

My face is deadpan. Then I can't help myself. I break out into a smile and start laughing.

"I'm onto you, Sure," Peter laughs. Then he gives me a high five and joins Allison Arnolds.

In the midst of all of this, Kathy and

Samantha Jenkins walk up to us. Kathy turns her tablet around so we can all see it.

"This is a draft of my latest article for *Right Next Door*," she says. "I wanted to run it by you all first."

WHAT?!

Listen, my middle school was just freed from a zombie epidemic, my mom's secret spy partner and octopus is speaking to us, and my older sister briefly drooled all over herself, but *Kathy Jenkins* asking to run an article by us *before publishing it* . . . that may just be the most unbelievable thing that's transpired so far.

I pinch myself. Nope. Definitely not dreaming. I glance at the headline.

SURE THINGS, INC. AND DEFINITE DEVICES
SAVE FILLMORE MIDDLE SCHOOL FROM EVIL,
MYSTERIOUS LUNCH MEAT
by Kathy Jenkins and Emily Sure

Emily's mouth drops open.
"You gave *me* credit?" she squeals.

"Of course," Kathy says. "You got the audio recording that solved the mystery and captured the facts. You did the investigative journalism. You deserve the credit. You did some excellent work, Emily. I know it's only the first week of school, but if you keep this up, I can see you becoming EDITOR-IN-CHIEF of the school paper someday. And maybe even a guest reporter for *Right Next Door!*"

Emily beams with pride. Mom does too. Even I'm feeling a little happy for Emily.

At that moment Jada taps me on the shoulder.

"Can we take a walk outside?" she asks.

I nod. I don't know why, especially after everything, but I feel kind of nervous. Jada and I step outside.

"You know, you really are an amazing inventor, Billy," Jada says. "None of this rescue would have been possible without you. I'm impressed."

"Well, you definitely have me beat in *Sandbox XXL*," I say. "And you were a big help in getting things back to normal here at Fillmore."

Jada smiles.

"And I thought the lunch at my school was bad," she says. We both share a laugh.

There's an awkward silence, almost like neither of us knows what to say. Then I notice we're both blushing. Remember when I said I like Jada? Well, I get the feeling that maybe, sorta, kinda . . . Jada likes me a little bit too.

I'm right. At that moment Jada leans in close and kisses me on the cheek! "What about Kevin?" I ask, which is something I've wanted to ask since the first day of school.

"Kevin?" Jada asks. "Oh, Billy. He's just my friend. I like YOU!"

My heart flutters. Jada—Jada likes ME?

Is this real? I find myself thinking.

We head back into the school.

"*Sandbox XXL* at the arcade next weekend?" I ask.

"You bet!" says Jada. "And I'll try my best to go easy on you!"

Once we're back inside the building, I take a look around. All at once I'm surrounded by my sister, my mom, my best friend and business partner, an octopus secret agent, a reporter that used to be my enemy who is now my friend, and all of my friends at Fillmore Middle School. Not to mention a girl I really, really like, who kind of, maybe, definitely likes me back. The only thing I'm missing are my dad and dog.

Just as I'm thinking that, a sensible sedan I know all too well shows up at the school.

"*Ruuuuf! arf! arf!*" comes a little dog's voice from the car.

It's Dad and Philo! And Manny's parents are in the back!

"We wanted to celebrate too," Dad says, and joins me for a hug. "We're all so proud of you, Billy."

"I have the best business partner in the world," Manny says next to me.

"You get one day free of homework, Mr. Sure," says Mr. Jennings.

Everyone joins in for a group hug.

Yeah, you know that first week of school feeling?

It feels pretty good right about now.

Here's to eighth grade!

Your shoulder's open," Grandpa Joe says for the 47,718th time of my twelve-year-long life. "Check yourself."

I sigh deeply into my glove so my grandfather won't hear me. It's annoying listening to those exact words *every single time* I practice with him. It's even more annoying knowing that he's usually right. Well, to be honest, more like *always* right.

Grandpa Joe lobs the ball back to me. I carefully move my fingers around the seams to get the right grip. I try to stop thinking about how annoyed I feel, and set my mind on my balance instead.

"Check your feet, kiddo," Grandpa reminds me.

Oh yeah, my feet. I set them into the position Grandpa taught me when I was barely big enough to hold a ball in my hand. I bend my knees so I'm loose, then I take a deep breath. Eyes focused on my target, I pull back into my balance point, hold my shoulder in line with my eyes, shift to power position, and throw the ball as hard as I can. It hits Grandpa's glove dead in the center with a loud *thwack!*

"There you go!" Grandpa cheers. "Who's on your side, Matt?"

"You are, Grandpa," I reply for the 47,718th time. "Always."

I hear the familiar sound of rugged tires crunching the gravel in our driveway. Have I mentioned that it's only 7:30 a.m.? And that I've been throwing a baseball for thirty minutes already? And that I still have a full day of school—and a play-off game—ahead of me? Welcome to the world of Matt Vezza. It's an exhausting place!

My best friend, Luis Ramirez, is sitting on his dirt bike, waiting for me to grab my stuff so we can ride to school together. He looks at me, grins, and shakes his head.

"Okay, I know you're a pretty good pitcher, but are you *ever* going to learn how to throw a baseball like your grandpa, dude?" Luis chuckles as he tips his bucket hat at my grandfather. "Morning, Grandpa Joe."

"Morning, Luis," Grandpa Joe replies.

Grandpa Joe tosses the ball to Luis. I put my head down and pretend to stare at the ground, because I know what's sure to come next when Luis tosses the ball back. Shoulder open, grip totally wrong, the ball flies wildly up over Grandpa Joe's head. He reaches up and grabs it like the pro ballplayer that he almost was, but I can see the pain flash through his face when he reaches down and rubs his ankle.

"Are you okay, Grandpa?" I say, trying to sound nonchalant, but concerned. I know Grandpa Joe's pain has been getting worse and worse, even though he's been trying to hide it.

"Okay? I've got more energy than you two combined!" Grandpa Joe says proudly. "And if *you* ever want to learn to throw a baseball, I'll be here waiting, Luis."

"Thanks, Grandpa Joe, but you know baseball's not my thing," Luis says with a laugh. He twirls his bucket hat on his finger for a moment and then tosses it in the air. It lands perfectly on his head. Even I have to admit, it's pretty impressive.

I give Grandpa a quick pat good-bye on the back, then hop on my bike. I know he loves me, but Grandpa isn't exactly the hugging type. He's old school in every way. I just wish I got a chance to see him when he was young.

"Grandpa Joe is mad cool," Luis yells to me. "But baseball? Dude, it is sooooo boring."

"It's only boring if you don't understand the game," I say, sounding like a Grandpa Joe clone. Sometimes I can't help myself. It's scary.

We ride up Park Street, make a left on Pine, and then hit Washington Avenue. Sands Middle School is standing proudly in the distance, eagerly awaiting our arrival.

"Hey, Matt, are you ready for . . . ," Luis calls as we race toward the bike rack. Then he makes a cone with his hands and shouts through it, "TRRRREEEEMMMMMT TIME?"

Luis is referring to Ms. Tremt, our school librarian. It's Wednesday, so we have library first period.

Ms. Tremt seems all right to me, but she's always been the subject of cafeteria gossip. It might be the furry, incredibly colorful scarves she likes to wear, even when it's eighty degrees outside. Or the boxes and boxes of library books that never seem to disappear, no matter how much unpacking we do for her. But most likely, it's the way she sits silently and stares at one student for nearly the entire period while we're reading. Which could seem totally creepy, except that after she stares at you for a while, Ms. Tremt always comes over and hands you a book that you fall in love with from the first paragraph, or the perfect book to help with your science report. It's like she's psychic or something.

"I'm actually looking forward to library today," I tell Luis.

"Oh no!" Luis gasps. "It's finally happened. My best friend has been invaded by AN ALIEN BODY SNATCHER!"

Luis grabs his throat and pretends like he's gasping for air. Then he tumbles to the floor.

"Always a comedian." I laugh. "I'm serious, though. Ms. Tremt said she was going to order me a book about New York baseball in 1951. I want to see if it came in yet. I never mentioned anything to her about 1951. Or New York. I just told her I'd like to read any books she had about baseball history and she chose that specific year and place. Weird."

"You and baseball." Luis sighs. "So much love. I just don't get it. And who cares about games played sixty years ago?"

I wait a second. Then I can practically see the lightbulb go off over Luis's head.

"Ohhhh . . . 1951 . . . *New York* baseball," he says. "Wasn't Grandpa Joe supposed to play for the Giants that year? Now I get it."

"Yup. 1951 . . . It was a great time to be a baseball fan in New York," I say. "You had three home teams to choose from—the New York Yankees, the New York Giants, or the Brooklyn Dodgers. And if you think the rivalry between the New York Mets and New York Yankees is fierce today, you should read about the rivalries back then! If you lived in Brooklyn, there was no way you could be a Yankees or Giants fan. You were a Dodgers fan all the way."

"And I'm guessing you want to learn more about what baseball was like in the time when Grandpa Joe almost made the major leagues?" Luis says.

"It takes you a while, but you're not nearly as clueless as you look," I say with a chuckle.

"Hey, leave the jokes to the professional," a voice says from behind me.

I turn around and see Grace Scott standing there, balancing a huge wobbly pile of books in her hands.

"I believe by professional, you are referring to me? Funny friend, at your service," Luis teases. "Just a little light reading, huh, Gracie?"

"A little," Grace replies. "I wanted to get Ms. Tremt's opinion on some of my favorite books. She always has great suggestions about what type of books I should be reading."

"Ms. Tremt wants our minds . . . and our *sooouls*," Luis says, doing the dramatic thing with his hand and voice again. "That's why she stares so deeply at us."

Luis is interrupted by the sound of the first bell. Sands Middle School is open for business. I grab a stack of Grace's books and hand them to Luis, then take a stack myself. We all know the pile will be scattered across the hallowed halls of our school if we leave them in Grace's hands. She's . . . um . . . how shall I put this? Working on improving her balancing skills at the moment. Actually, more like for the past twelve years.

(Don't ever tell Grace I told you this, but in second grade, a couple of mean kids started calling her "Grace-less" behind her back. Luis and I put a stop to that—real fast. We may seem like an odd bunch of bananas, as my grandpa would say, but a friend is a friend. And *nobody* messes with one of our friends.)

After a quick homeroom check-in, we race down the hall and stagger into the library twelve seconds before the first-period bell rings.

Ms. Tremt's scarf is particularly furry today and a shade of green that I have never seen before in my life. It looks almost like a caterpillar . . . a vibrating, furry caterpillar . . . a vibrating, furry, *hungry* caterpillar, just like the one in my favorite book when I was a little . . . Wait, what? Is Ms. Tremt's scarf hypnotizing me or something? That's so weird.

"Matthew," Ms. Tremt says, smiling as she hands me a book. "I believe you were waiting for this?"

"Huh?" I say, still wondering where the whole caterpillar trail of thought came from.

Then I take a look at the book. *It Was the Shot Heard 'Round the World: The Amazing Story of the 1951 Giants-Dodgers Pennant Race.* Perfect!

Looking for another great book?
Find it
IN THE MIDDLE.

Fun, fantastic books for kids in the in-beTWEEN age.

IntheMiddleBooks.com

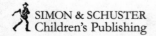